RANDOM HOUSE
CHILDREN'S BOOKS
A DIVISION OF RANDOM HOUSE, INC.

TITLE: My Name Is Mina

AUTHOR: David Almond

IMPRINT: Delacorte Press

PUBLICATION DATE: October 11, 2011

ISBN: 978-0-385-74073-9

PRICE: $15.99 U.S./$17.99 CAN.

GLB ISBN: 978-0-375-98964-3

GLB PRICE: $18.99 U.S./$20.99 CAN.

EBOOK ISBN: 978-0-375-98965-0

EBOOK PRICE: $15.99 U.S./$15.99 CAN.

PAGES: 304

AGES: 10 & up

MY NAME is MINA

ALSO BY DAVID ALMOND

My NAME is MINA

DAVID ALMOND

Delacorte Press

Text copyright © 2010 by David Almond
Jacket art copyright © 2010 by David McDougall

Visit us on the Web! www.randomhouse.com/kids

Educators and librarians, for a variety of teaching tools, visit us at
www.randomhouse.com/teachers

Library of Congress Cataloging-in-Publication Data
Almond, David.
  My name is Mina / David Almond. — Hardcover trade ed.
    p. cm.
  Prequel to: Skellig.
  Summary: Creative, intelligent, nine-year-old Mina keeps a journal in her
own disorderly way that reveals how her mind is growing into something
extraordinary, especially after she begins homeschooling under the direction of
her widowed mother.
  ISBN 978-0-385-74073-9 (hardcover) — ISBN 978-0-375-98964-3 (glb) —
ISBN 978-0-375-98965-0 (ebook)
[1. Eccentrics and eccentricities—Fiction. 2. Home schooling—Fiction.
3. Mothers and daughters—Fiction. 4. Single-parent families—Fiction. 5. Family
life—England—Fiction. 6. England—Fiction.] I. Title.
PZ7.A448Myn 2011
[Fic]—dc22
2010040143

Text design by David McDougall
Printed in the United States of America
10 9 8 7 6 5 4 3 2 1
First American Edition

For Sara Jane and Freya

MOONLIGHT, WONDER, FLIES & NONSENSE

My name is Mina and I love the night. Anything seems possible at night when the rest of the world has gone to sleep. It's dark and silent in the house, but if I listen close, I hear the beat beat beat of my heart. I hear the creak and crack of the house. I hear my mum breathing gently in her sleep in the room next door.

I slip out of bed and sit at the table by the window. I tug the curtain open. There's a full moon in the middle of the sky. It bathes the world in its silvery light. It shines on Falconer Road and on the houses and the streets beyond, and on the city roofs and spires and on the distant mountains and moors. It shines into the room and onto me.

Some say that you should turn your face from the light of the moon. They say it makes you mad.

I turn my face towards it and I laugh.

Make me mad, I whisper. Go on, make Mina mad.

I laugh again.

Some people think that she's already mad, I think.

I look into the night. I see owls and bats that fly and flicker across the moon. Somewhere out there, Whisper the cat is slipping through the shadows. I close my eyes and it's like those creatures are moving inside me, almost like I'm a kind of weird creature myself, a girl whose name is Mina but more than just a girl whose name is Mina.

There's an empty notebook lying on the table in the moonlight. It's been there for an age. I keep on saying that I'll write a journal. So I'll start right here, right now. I open the book and write the very first words:

MY NAME is MINA AND I LOVE THE NIGHT.

Then what shall I write? I can't just write that this happened then this happened then this happened to boring infinitum. I'll let my journal grow just like the mind does, just like a tree or a beast does, just like life does. Why should a book tell a tale in a dull straight line?

Words should wander and meander. They should fly like owls and flicker like bats and slip like cats. They should murmur and scream and dance and sing.

Sometimes there should be no words at all.

Just silence.

Just clean white space.

Some pages will be like a sky with a single bird in it. Some will be like a sky with a swirling swarm of starlings in it. My sentences will be a clutch, a collection, a pattern, a swarm, a shoal, a mosaic. They will be a circus, a menagerie, a tree, a nest. Because my mind is not in order. My mind is not straight lines. My mind is a clutter and a mess. It is my mind, but it is also very like other minds. And like all minds, like every mind that there

has ever been and every mind that there will
ever be, it is a place of wonder.

!THE MIND IS A PLACE OF WONDER!

THE MIND IS

!THE MIND IS A PLACE OF WONDER!

A PLACE OF

!THE MIND IS A PLACE OF WONDER!

WONDER

!THE MIND IS A PLACE OF WONDER!

When I was at school — at St. Bede's Middle —
I was told by my teacher Mrs. Scullery that I
should not write anything until I had planned what
I would write. What nonsense!

Do I plan a sentence before I speak it?
OF COURSE I DO NOT!
Does a bird plan its song before it sings?
OF COURSE IT DOES NOT!
It opens its beak and it
SINGS so I will SING!

I did want to be what they called a good girl, so I did try. There was one fine morning when the sun was shining through the classroom window. There was a cloud of flies shimmering and dancing in the air outside. I heard Mrs. Scullery telling us that she wanted us to write a story. Of course we'd need to write a plan first, she said.

She asked us whether we understood.

We told her that we did.

So I stopped staring at the flies (which I had been enjoying very much!), and I wrote my plan. My story would have such and such a title, and would begin in such and such a way, then such and such would happen in the middle, then such and such would be the outcome at the end.

I wrote it all down very neatly.

I showed my plan to Mrs. Scullery, and she was very pleased. She even smiled at me and said, "Well done, Mina. That is very good, dear. Now you may write the story."

But of course when I started to write, the story wouldn't keep still, wouldn't obey. The words danced like flies. They flew off in strange and beautiful directions and took my story on a very unexpected course. I was very pleased with it, but when I showed it to Mrs. Scullery, she just got cross. She held the plan in one hand and the story in the other.

"They do not match!" she said in her screechy voice.

"I don't know what you mean, Miss," I said.

She leaned down towards me.

"The story," she said, in a slow stupid voice like she was talking to somebody slow and stupid, "does not fit the plan!"

"But it didn't want to, Miss," I answered.

"Didn't want to? What on earth do you mean, it didn't want to?"

"I mean it wanted to do other things, Miss."

She put her hands on her hips and shook her head. "It is a story," she said. "It is your story. It will do what you tell it to."

"But it won't," I said. She kept on glaring at me.

"And Miss," I said, like I was pleading with her to understand. "I don't want it to, Miss."

I should have saved my breath. She flung the papers onto my table.

"This is typical of you," she said. "Absolutely typical!"

And she turned to a girl called Samantha and asked her to read her tale, which was something about a girl with curly hair and her cuddly cat, a perfectly planned idiotic thing in which nothing interesting happened at all! And of course all the other kids were giggling through it all, and it led to one of the nicknames I had back then. Typical. Absolutely Typical McKee.

Huh! Huh! Typical!

My stories were like me. They couldn't be controlled and they couldn't fit in. Trying to be a good girl sometimes made me very sad. The end of it all was the day I became nonsensical. Fantastically nonsensical. I'll tell the story of that day when the time seems right, when the words seem right. And I suppose I'll tell the other tales that matter, like the tale of my day at Corinthian Avenue and my vision, or the story of my journey to the Underworld in Heston Park, or the story of my grandfather's house and the owls. And I'll put in poems and scribblings and nonsense. Sometimes writing nonsense can make a lot of sense! That sounds nonsensical itself, of course, but it isn't. **NON-SENS-I-CAL! WHAT A GREAT WORD! WOW!**

NONSENSICAL!

Now I've started, it's lovely to see the empty pages that stretch before me. Writing will be like a journey, every word a footstep that takes me further into an undiscovered land.

Look at the way the words move across the page and fill the empty spaces. Did God feel like this when he started to fill the emptiness? Is there a God? Was there ever emptiness? I don't know, but it doesn't stop me wondering and wondering.*

*Wandering and wondering are almost the same word. And wandering through space is very like wondering inside the head. I am a wonderer and a wanderer!

Sometimes I look at the world and I'm amazed that there's anything at all.

WHY IS THERE ANYTHING?
WHY IS THERE SOMETHING,
RATHER THAN NOTHING?
WHY? WHY? WHY? WHY?
AND BEFORE THERE WAS
S O M E T H I N G,
WAS THERE JUST NOTHING?
AND DID THAT NOTHING
TURN INTO SOMETHING?
AND IF THAT NOTHING
TURNED INTO SOMETHING,
HOW DID IT DO IT, AND
WHY? WHY? WHY? WHY?

My motto's written on paper and pinned
above my bed:

How can a bird that is born for joy
Sit in a cage and sing?

It's by William Blake. Blake the Misfit, Blake the
Outsider. Just like me. He was a painter and a poet
and some people said he was mad — just like they
say about me. Maybe he was out too much in the
moon. Sometimes he wore no clothes. Sometimes he
saw angels in his garden. He saw spirits all around
him. I think he was very sane. So does my mum,
so did my dad. I will write with William Blake in
mind. I will write about the sad things, of course,
because there is no way not to write about the sad
things. And there are sad things in my life. Well,
ONE BIG SAD AND HORRIBLE THING.
Weirdly enough, the sad things in my life make the
happy things seem more intense. I wonder if other
people feel like that, if they feel that sadness, in a
weird way, can help to make you more intensely

happy. That's what's known as a paradox, I suppose.

PARADOX!

What a word! It sounds good, looks good, and the meaning's good! And if something is a paradox, it is PARADOXICAL. Which is an even better word!

PARADOXICAL!

That's the kind of nickname I'd like to have. Not Typical McKee, but Paradoxical McKee!

Or Nonsensical McKee, of course.

Anyway, I'll try to make my words break out of the cages of sadness, and make them sing for joy.

Suddenly, thinking about the **ONE BIG SAD AND HORRIBLE THING,** I know that I'm writing all this for Dad. I imagine him watching me and reading my words as I write. He'll be everywhere in this journal, of course, in my mind and in my words and moving among the spaces between the words and behind the words. Sometimes

I tell people that he died before I was born, but that isn't true, and I do have some memories of him. I'll write of those. I think of him watching from somewhere far away beyond the moon. Hello, Dad. Yes, I think I'm happy now. Yes, I think Mum is, too. Good night.

I slip back into bed. The maddening moon shines down on me. I've started the journal at last. Tomorrow I'll write some more. Now I'll try to dream of bats and cats and owls.

BANANAS, WEIRDOS, A BEAUTIFUL TREE & BORING HEAVEN

Had breakfast with Mum. Bananas and yogurt and toast with marmalade. DELICIOUS! I told her I'd started my journal. Excellent, she said. I said I might show her some of the pages when I'm ready. Excellent, she said. She said maybe we could make some clay models today. Excellent, I said. Then I came out of the house and climbed into my tree, and here I am.

I love my tree. I've been climbing it for a couple of years. I shin up the trunk to a branch that's just a bit higher than my head. I sit here astride the branch with my back against the trunk. Sometimes I let my legs dangle. Sometimes I sit with my knees raised so that I can rest a book on them. It's very comfortable, like it was made for me. I've been known to sit here for hours at a time, drawing or reading, or just thinking and looking and listening and wondering.

It's early spring. A pair of blackbirds are building a nest, not too far away from me. The nest's almost done. I know that because I sometimes climb higher and look down into it. One day soon I'll look down and see eggs in there. Then

23

I'll see chicks. Then I'll see fledglings leaving the nest. Then I'll see the fledglings become birds that fly into the blue blue yonder. How amazing is that? The blackbirds squawk alarm calls when I climb higher, like they're yelling, 'Behave yourself! Squawk! Get back down, girl! Squawk!' But I don't think they're really too troubled by me, not like they would be by a cat, for instance, or by a stranger. Maybe they think I'm some kind of weird bird myself, or some kind of peculiar branch. Maybe if I sat very still for a very long time, they'd build a nest in me: in my lap, or in my hair, or in my hands if I raised them up and cupped them. There is a story about this called St. Kevin and the Blackbird.

ST. KEVIN AND THE BLACKBIRD

LONG AGO, THERE WAS A SAINT CALLED KEVIN WHO LIVED IN IRELAND. ONE DAY, HE WAS PRAYING WITH HIS HANDS STRETCHED TOWARDS HEAVEN (OR WHAT HE THOUGHT WAS HEAVEN), WHEN A BLACKBIRD FLEW DOWN AND LAID AN EGG IN HIS HANDS. ST. KEVIN WAS A GOOD MAN, AND HE DIDN'T WANT TO BREAK THE EGG OR PREVENT IT FROM HATCHING — AND BEING A SAINT, HE ALSO PROBABLY THOUGHT THAT THE EGG WAS A GIFT FROM GOD. SO HE STAYED IN EXACTLY THE SAME POSITION FOR DAY AFTER DAY AND NIGHT AFTER NIGHT, WITH HIS HANDS STRETCHED TOWARDS HEAVEN (OR WHAT HE THOUGHT WAS HEAVEN), UNTIL THE EGG HATCHED RIGHT THERE IN HIS HANDS. IMAGINE THAT, A TINY CHICK MAKING ITS FIRST MOVEMENTS IN YOUR HANDS. IMAGINE THE CLAWS, THE WET WINGS, THE CHEEP CHEEP CHEEP. IMAGINE IT GROWING AS YOU CARED FOR IT. AND IMAGINE IT FLYING AWAY!

Some of the kids from St. Bede's passed by the end of the street a few moments back. They saw me, but they've stopped laughing and calling by now. These days they just roll their eyes and whisper a few words to each other and head onto the gates of their cage. That's if they do anything at all. They used to call me a **witch and a weirdo.** They yelled I was a **monkey and a crow.** They had great fun last year. In the summer they threw daisies and yelled, **"Daisies for Miss Crazy!"** In the autumn they threw conkers and yelled, **"Conkers for Miss Bonkers!"** (Which is quite amusing when you think about it, I suppose.)

Now I'm just part of the scenery, like I am for the birds. I am like a lamppost or a tree or a stone. I don't care. They're nothing to me. I don't even look at them. Them! Huh! HUH! Nothing!

This is Falconer Road. It's a narrow street of terraced houses with little front gardens, each garden with a single tree in it, like this one. The houses are perhaps eighty years old. There are back lanes and garages behind the houses. Beyond the end of the street is Crow Road, where the bigger older houses are. I own a house there, or I will when I'm grown up. It is a bit dilapidated and has extraordinary creatures living in it. Thank you, Grandpa. I raise my eyes to the sky. Thank you, Grandpa. He left it to me in his will. He's another one that's dead. We say he's in Heaven with Dad.

Heaven. I used to think that the idea of Heaven was silly. I used to think of all the people who keep on dying. Heaven must get ridiculously full, I thought. There wouldn't be room anywhere in the universe for it.

"How big is Heaven?" I said to Mum one day when I was small. I'd just seen a hearse with a coffin in it heading past the end of the street to the massive cemetery on Jesmond Road, the one where Dad's buried.

"Oh, very very big, I should think," she said.

I thought of all the cemeteries in all the world. I thought of all the people lying in them. I thought of all the people who have lived and died in the years and years and years of time. I just couldn't imagine it.

"It must be ginormous," I said.

"Yes, I suppose so," she said.

Then, a few weeks later, we were reading an encyclopedia. It said that if you counted all the people who had ever lived in all the history of the world until about fifty years ago, there wouldn't be as many as the people who are alive today.*

- That surprised us a great deal.

It was a couple of hours later that I realized what that meant.

"So that means," I said, "that Heaven only needs to be about as big as the earth."

"Yes," she said. "I suppose that's true."

And we laughed about it, because compared with the size of the universe, earth isn't very big at all. And even earth isn't full. There's room for lots more bodies, just like in Heaven there's room for lots more souls.

These days, though, I don't believe any of that. I think that the idea of Heaven is silly for other reasons. When people try to say what Heaven

***

* Extraordinary Fact! There are as many people alive in the world today as there have been in the whole of human history!

is like, it just sounds deadly deadly deadly dull. Standing around singing and eating nectar or something and looking at God and praising him and being very very very good. Imagine that! **YAWN YAWN YAWN YAWN!** Who'd want to do that for century after century after century after century? Somebody like Mrs. Scullery, maybe, but not me. I bet that even the angels get fed up with it all. I bet they want to eat bananas and marmalade and chocolate, and to look at things like clouds of flies, and to climb trees or to play with cats. I bet they look at us and envy us for being human. I bet that sometimes they even want to be like us. Except they might get put off by the fact that we die.

Anyway, in the end, I don't really believe in Heaven at all, and I don't believe in perfect angels. I think that this might be the only Heaven there can possibly be, this world we live in now, but we haven't quite realized it yet. And I think that the only possible angels might be us.

THIS MIGHT BE HEAVEN!
WE MIGHT BE LIVING
IN HEAVEN RIGHT NOW!
AND WE MIGHT BE THE ANGELS!

Is that stupid? No, it's not! Look at the blackbird, the way the sunlight glistens on it. Look at the way it shimmers, the way its blackness glints with silver, purple, green, and even white beneath the sun. Listen to its song. Look at the way it jumps into the sky. Look how the leaves are coming out from the buds. Feel how strong the tree is and feel the beat of my heart and the sun on my skin and the air on my cheek. Think of things like the human voice, the solar system, the fur of a cat, the sea, bananas, a duck-billed platypus. Look at the things that we've made: houses and pavements and walls and steeples and roads and cars and, songs and poems, and yes I know that it's a long long way from being perfect. But perfection would be very dull and perfection isn't the point.

!PERFECTION IS BORING!
!PERFECTION IS EMPTY!
!PERFECTION IS NOTHINGNESS!

Look at the world. Smell it, taste it, listen to it, feel it, look at it. Look at it! And I know horrible things happen for no good reason. Why did my dad die? What's the point of famine and fear and darkness and war? I don't know! I'm just a kid! How can I know answers to things like that? But this horrible world is so blooming beautiful and so blooming weird that sometimes I think it'll make me faint!

JUST LOOK AT
THE MIND-BLOWING LIP-SMACKING
WONDERFUL AMAZING BEAUTIFUL
STUNNING MARVELOUS GORGEOUS

Lovely loveliness

OF OUR WORLD!

"Mina!" calls Mum. "Mina!"

"Coming, Mum!"

I don't move.

There's a white van at Mr. Myers's house just along the street. He died. (Another one! It's about time we had some people born around here!) He was called Ernie and he was very old. He used to stand at his window staring out and even when you smiled and waved at him, you couldn't be certain if he'd seen you, or if he thought he was dreaming about you. I used to wonder what was going on inside his brain. Did he see the same things as everybody else, or did he see different things? Did he see nothing at all? Did the world, and me and everybody in it, seem like a dream? And come to that, do any of us see what another person sees? Maybe we're all living in some strange kind of dream. If we are, of course, we don't know that we are.

I used to see a doctor going into the house sometimes. He was a miserable-looking gray kind of bloke that came in a miserable-looking gray kind of car. He caught sight of me in the tree one day. I started to wave but he just scowled, like he thought that sitting in a tree was the stupidest thing in the whole wide world. It was obviously far too much of a struggle for somebody like him to smile and wave back at somebody like me. Huh. Wouldn't want him to be my doctor. He'd make you feel like topping yourself just by looking at you. Can't have been much of a doctor, anyway. Mr. Myers died, and was dead for nearly a week before they found him, lying under the table in the kitchen. Poor soul. He had a daughter, but I don't think she ever really cared for him. She's at the house right now, carrying out some of Mr. Myers's belongings to the van. She's another streak of misery. She was like that even when Ernie was alive. Maybe she thought he'd have some gold hidden away, rather than old table lamps and worn rugs and tatty chairs that she's carrying out now. Mum says the place is full of stuff, piled up in the attic and in the dilapidated garage at the back of the house.

Look at her. Misery Guts. You had him until he was old! You had your dad till he was old and you didn't care!

The streak of misery's putting Mr. Myers's house up for sale. Wonder who'll buy it.

"Mina!"

"Yes, Mum!"

"Mina!"

Listen to how lovely her voice is. Call again, Mum.

"Mina!"

Wow.

"Yes, Mum!"

DINOSAURS,

FRENCH TOAST

& A JOURNEY

IN THE

UNDERWORLD

We made animals at the kitchen table for much of the day. I started with a worm then a snake then a rat then a cat then a dog then a cow then a horse then a hippopotamus. I made an imaginary creature with wings and claws. I made a baby and rocked it in my hands and sang a lullaby to it. I squashed the clay together and started again and I made an archaeopteryx.

The archaeopteryx was a dinosaur, a dinosaur with wings and feathers. It could fly. Probably not as well as birds can now. It was a bony thing, and probably just made short sharp clumsy flights. But it didn't die out. It was the only dinosaur that survived, and it's the ancestor of all the birds that exist in the world today. The blackbirds building their nest in the tree above my head are its descendants!

There are archaeopteryx fossils in the Natural History Museum in London. Mum has said we'll go to see them, when she has a bit of time, and a bit of money.

She smiled as she watched me molding the clay.
"Archaeopteryx," she said. "Isn't it a lovely word?"
"Yes."

ARCHAEOPTERYX! ARK-Y-OPT-ER-IX.
ARCHAEOPTERYX!

I love sticking my fingers into the clay, bending it and shaping it, ripping it and thumping it and rolling it and squashing it. I love smoothing it with water. I love the way it dries to a crust on your skin and then the way it cracks when you make a fist, the way it turns to dust. I love the way it dries out in the oven. We can't afford a proper kiln, so the things we make go in with loaves of bread and casseroles and pizzas and curries, so they never get properly baked or properly glazed. That doesn't matter to us. We think they're beautiful. We paint them, and we put them on the shelves around us. Sometimes we make little models of each other. Mum has made a little model of Dad — it looks nothing like him, of course, at least not when I compare it with his photographs, but somehow it seems to be more like him than the photographs do.*

While we were working the clay, I remembered a day when I was small (funny how writing like this makes me keep thinking about what

*This makes me think about how some people say that "modern" art can't be much good because it doesn't much look like anything in the world. But maybe it's not trying to look like the world. Maybe it's trying to be like the world. Or maybe trying to do a kind of impossible thing — to look like something that's in the world but can't really be seen at all.

I was like when I was small) and still at school.
There was an Art lesson and I got carried away.
We were using plasticine in Mrs. Tompkinson's Art
class and I made a little man. I made him walk
along my desk. When I thought nobody was looking
I picked him up and started whispering into his ear.

"Come alive!" I whispered. "Come alive!"

I concentrated very hard, trying to make him
come alive.

There was a boy at the next table (Joseph
Simm? I can't remember. I tried very hard to put
them all out of my brain). I caught him looking at
me. I stared back like I was asking him, "What do
you think you're looking at?" He shook his head like
he thought I was crazy. I pointed a finger at him
and waggled it and I rolled my eyes like I was
putting a spell on him.

"Please, Miss!" he called. "Mina McKee's
being weird again."

Weird! Huh! HUH!

When we'd finished working the clay, we washed our
hands and had French toast with cinnamon on it.

TOTALLY TOTALLY DELICIOUS. My mum is a fantastic cook! We went out for a walk. I told Mum about the blackbirds' nest and about Mr. Myers's daughter. His house looked so dirty and dark as we passed by it.

"Wonder who'll buy it," I said.

"Somebody who doesn't mind getting their hands dirty," she said. "Somebody who can imagine how it'll be when it's all done up."

We walked to Heston Park. We passed very close to the entrance to the Underworld. I quaked inside, and I must have trembled or twitched or something, because Mum came to a halt.

"Are you OK, Mina?" she asked.

The locked steel gate was close behind her.

"Yes, Mum," I said.

"Are you certain?"

"Yes, Mum."

I wondered if I should tell her the tale of the day I went through the steel gate all alone. I didn't. When I think about it, there's quite a few things I don't tell her about. Like most kids, I suppose. Sometimes it's best just to keep things to myself because I don't want to upset her. Sometimes they're just too weird to explain. Sometimes I just don't know how to get the words out. It doesn't matter. I guess she knows there's lots of things she doesn't know about me. But it doesn't matter. You don't have to know every single thing about a person in order to understand them.

She smiled and hugged me.

"You're a strange one," she said as we walked on.

"I know," I said.

I'll write the story of the Underworld for her and maybe I'll let her read it. Somehow it might make more sense if it's written down.

Night. Even at night the city rumbles and roars. Traffic drones on the motorway that circles the center. There are machines and engines that can never be allowed to rest. And even the breathing and snoring and whispering must add to the din. And the running of water through pipes, and the humming of electricity, and the chatter of televisions watched by people who can't sleep, and dogs that bark and cats that yowl. And there are the owls, as always, hooting as they fly over Crow Road and Heston Park. Hello, Owls. Hoot. Hoot. I try to hoot like an owl but it sounds nothing like an owl.

I thought I'd write the story of the Underworld in the first person, and say, "I did this and I did that." But somehow it's better to write this in the third person, to say, "Mina did this and Mina did that." I write it by moonlight, to the hooting of the owls.

MINA IN THE UNDERWORLD

She was just nine years old. She was very skinny and very small and she had jet-black hair and a pale pale face and shining eyes. Some folks said she was weird. Her mum said she was brave. Sometimes she seemed very old for her age, and sometimes she seemed just like a little girl. All those things were true. She felt so strong and bold, lonely and lost, and the world seemed very big and she seemed very small. Her mum said that everybody felt like that at some time in their lives, no matter how old they were, but that for Mina it was more difficult because of what had happened to her dad. She said that as Mina grew, she'd feel stronger more often and not feel so small.

Mina's mum was strong. To Mina she seemed brave and gentle. She had glossy red hair and dark green eyes and Mina thought that if there was such a thing as a saint in this world, then her mum was one.

In the past, Mina had heard her mother arguing with doctors, especially with the doctor who talked about giving pills to Mina, pills that he said would make her feel better.

"They won't make her feel better!" said Mina's mum. "They'll stop her from feeling anything at all. She's not some kind of robot. She's a little girl that's growing up and she can do that without your stupid pills!"

Mina's school was St. Bede's Middle, very close to the park. It was a Monday morning in spring. The lesson was called History. The teacher, Mr. Henderson, talked about the city's past. He said that once the city had been surrounded by coal mines. For hundreds of years, men and boys had gone down into the earth to dig out coal. Imagine that, he said. He laughed. Imagine going into the pitch darkness to bring out stuff as black and bright as Mina McKee's hair. He said that if they could travel into the earth beneath the classroom, they would discover a warren of shafts and tunnels. His eyes widened. They might even discover the bones of those who had died down there. He said that the days of the coal mines had been very perilous, but people had lived and worked together, and shared their tragedies and joys.

He read some poems about pitmen, and played their songs on a CD player. He sang some pitmen's songs himself. He said that his own grandfather had been a pitman, and that he had been brought up with tales of the underground, of the men who traveled deep into the earth every day, of ponies they had down there, and of the ghosts they said they had seen down there.

He showed them maps of the city as it used to be. There were pit shafts that plunged hundreds of feet down into the earth. There were tunnels that crept from the city's fringes towards its heart. He said that very close to the school, in Heston Park, there was an entrance to tunnel that once was used to carry carts of coal from the coal mines down to the river. He said the tunnel was being repaired. There were plans to reopen it for tourists and for those who wanted to study the city's past. Maybe when it opened, he said, they'd all go into the tunnel together on a class trip. Then the lesson ended.

Mina already knew about the entrance and the tunnel. She'd seen the ancient solid steel gate behind some rhododendron bushes. She'd seen the girders welded across the gate. Recently, she'd seen that the girders had gone. Men wearing hard hats and carrying big torches went into it. There was a new orange sign there. It said DANGER KEEP OUT and there was a skull and crossbones symbol on it.

In Mina's mind, the gate, the tunnel, and now Mr. Henderson's stories mingled with many other stories that she'd heard — stories from ancient times about heroes and heroines who lived in the underground: Daedalus, who built an underground maze with a monster called the Minotaur at its heart; Pluto, the King of the

Underworld, and Persephone, his wife; stories about the dead, who were taken from this world to live in the darkness below. And they mingled with the tale of Orpheus, the greatest singer in the world, whose beautiful wife, Eurydice, was killed by a venomous snake. Orpheus would not accept her death. He traveled the world, searching for the entrance to the Underworld. When he found it, he went down into the Underworld, and begged for her to be given back to him.

Mina knew it was silly, but she was only nine years old, and she was often very sad, and in her imagination and in her dreams, the entrance to the Underworld was there, behind the rhododendron bushes, in Heston Park. And she told herself she'd dare to go through that entrance. She'd go down to the Underworld like Orpheus did. He didn't manage to bring Eurydice back. But Mina would succeed. She'd go down. She'd meet Pluto and Persephone. She'd persuade them to let her bring her dad back into the world.

It happened the following Monday, jus

after the next of Mr. Henderson's History lessons.
At the end of the lesson, he stood in front of them
and started to sing.

"Lie doon, my dear, and in your ear,
To help you close your eye,
I'll sing a song, a slumber song,
A miner's lullaby.

"Coorie doon, Coorie doon, Coorie doon, my darling,
Coorie doon the day.
Coorie doon, Coorie Doon, Coorie doon, my darling,
Coorie doon the day."

Mr. Henderson paused for a moment.
    "Coorie doon means to snuggle down," he said.
"My grandpa sang this song to me to help to sleep
when I was a bairn. Imagine me as a bairn! And
imagine my tough old tender grandpa singing at
my side."
    He sang on. He ignored the stupid ignorant
kids that rolled their eyes and giggled, especially
the stupid ignorant boys that thought they were

so tough. And as he sang, Mina closed her eyes and imagined that the singing voice was her dad's.

"Your daddy's doon the mine, my darling,
Doon in the Curbly Main,
Your daddy's howkin coal, my darling,
For his own wean.

"Coorie doon, Coorie doon, Coorie doon, my darling,
Coorie doon the day.

"There's darkness doon the mine, my darling,
Darkness, dust and damp,
But we must have our heat, our light,
Our fire and our lamp.

"Coorie doon, Coorie doon, Coorie doon, my darling,
Coorie doon the day.

"Your daddy coories doon, my darling,
Doon in the three-foot seam,
So you can coorie doon, my darling,
Coorie doon and dream."

Mr. Henderson smiled as he wiped his eyes.

"You must always remember," he said, "the men and boys that dug out the stuff as black and bright as Mina McKee's hair."

That lunchtime the kids in the yard were rotten to her. They laughed like hyenas and called her Coaly McKee and Teacher's Pet and told her to get herself back to the underground where she belonged. She clenched her fists.

"You stupid bloody hyenas!" she said.

"Ooooh!" they said. "Mina McKee's swearing! I'm going to tell the teacher!"

"You are!" she yelled. "You're bloody stupid bloody hyenas!"

And she ran straight out of the school gate and into Heston Park. She slowed down. She listened for footsteps behind. She listened for her name being called, but there was nothing. A few men sprawled on a grass verge in the sunshine, reading newspapers and eating sandwiches. Their hard hats lay on the ground at their sides. They hardly looked up as Mina walked by. She walked towards the rhododendron bushes, then through them towards the steel gate. A stone had been put against the gate, but it was open, just a few inches. Mina looked at the skull and crossbones and quickly looked away. She was a small thin girl. She only needed to ease the gate open a few more inches, and she slithered inside.

Yes, it was very dark, but there was a pale light dangling close to her head. It lit steep steps that headed down into the earth. She followed them, twenty crumbling steps or more. Then she was in the tunnel itself, where another bulb dangled, and more bulbs dangled in the distance, showing the tunnel that stretched away to right and left. It was higher than her head. There was rubble on the tunnel floor, and a trickle of water. There was the stench of damp and rot and of what she thought must be death. She thought of the sun shining brightly in the outside world so nearby, and she had to tell herself not to run back up there in fright. She thought of Orpheus and of her father. She thought of the stupid hyena kids. None of them would dare to do something like this! She took a deep breath, and steeled herself, and headed down into the earth. She kept stumbling on the rubble, stretching out to steady herself on the damp walls. She kept expecting her voice to be called but there was nothing.

"My name is Mina," she kept on whispering, and her words echoed back to her. "My name is Mina. I am very brave."

There was a dull roaring sound from far away. She stopped and listened. Maybe it was water, or could it be the yelling and groaning of the dead?

"My name is Mina. I am very brave. My name is . . ."

Something brushed against her leg. She leapt away and screamed in horror and looked down and it was a black cat, weaving its way around her legs.

"A cat!" she gasped. "A cat!"

She couldn't stop shuddering as she leaned down to it. She stroked its dense dark fur and felt the heat of its body and she began to be soothed and calmed.

"My name is Mina," she whispered, and the cat mewed and purred in reply, and Mina knew she'd found a friend down here in the dark.

She moved on with the cat at her side. In places the walls of the tunnel had broken. Stones and bricks lay in untidy heaps. She imagined the world above, and the thickening layer of earth, stones, soil, bones, roots between herself and it. She imagined the whole tunnel collapsing onto her, as the tunnels could collapse onto pitmen long ago.

And then there was a ditch, crossing the route of the tunnels. By the frail light of the dangling bulb, she saw the stream rushing through the ditch. Mina caught her breath. She stroked the cat. This must be the river that Orpheus had to cross, the river between the world of the living and the dead. Suddenly, the cat drew back. There was a growling, and on the other side of the stream two eyes had begun to shine. This, thought Mina, is the monster, the guardian of the Underworld, that Orpheus had to tame.

It came closer, and showed itself to be a shaggy, thickset dog that snarled at them across the ditch.

Mina crouched down. She held out a friendly hand towards the dog, and in a trembling voice she started to sing, just like Orpheus did so long ago.

"Lie doon, my dear, and in your ear,
To help you close your eye,
I'll sing a song, a slumber song,
A miner's lullaby.

"Coorie doon, Coorie doon, Coorie doon, my darling,
Coorie doon the day."

The dog growled more softly. The cat came back to Mina's side. Mina went on singing and the dog lay down, as if it was asleep. Mina looked along the tunnel, which seemed to slope away endlessly. She was about to cross when there came a bellowing.

"Jasper!"

The dog stood up. Its ears twitched. It growled.

"Jasper! Where the hell you got to?"

There was a shadow far down in the tunnel, a deep dark shadow in the shape of a man.

"Jasper!"

The dog turned, and headed down towards the shadow.

"Who's that?" the shadow called. A deep cruel-sounding voice that boomed and echoed off the tunnel walls. "Is somebody there? Show yourself if you're there!"

Mina crouched low. She slithered back up the tunnel, keeping low, trying to keep her feet silent. Beyond a pile of fallen stones she stood up and ran.

"Who the hell is it?" yelled the shadow's voice. "What are you? What do you want down here?"

Mina kept on running, stumbling, reaching out to steady herself on the walls. The dog barked, the shadow called. In Mina's mind these were the voices of the dead and of a guardian monster. She could hear heavy thudding footsteps coming after her. She came to the foot of the ancient crumbling steps. She climbed them swiftly, slid through the steel gate into the sunlight again. She pushed it shut. The black cat disappeared through the rhododendrons. She went through them herself. The men still lay on the grass verge, still ate sandwiches and read newspapers, as if she'd been gone from the world just a few short moments. Again, they hardly looked at her as she passed close by. Her heart thundered as she tried to stay calm, to stay ordinary, to stop herself from bolting in fright.

And then there came first the screeching voice of Mrs. Malone, followed by Mrs. Malone herself striding through the park gate.

"Mina McKee! Mina McKee! Get yourself here this instant!"

Mr. Henderson was behind her. He was much more calm.

"Come back, Mina," he said. "Come back and we can all talk about it."

Mina's mum was called in, of course. They all stood in Mrs. Malone's office. It was the kids in the class, said Mina. It was the way they looked at her and the way they spoke to her. What was all the dirt on her? Why were her shoes so scuffed? She didn't know, she said. She told them that she had just been walking in the park, that she had climbed a tree. How could she tell them that she had gone like Orpheus in search of the Underworld? How could she tell them that she had charmed the guardian of the Underworld with her singing just like he did? How could she tell them that she had failed to bring back her loved one just like he did? How could she tell them that the gates to the Underworld could be found in Heston Park?

In the end she just said,

"All I did was to run away for a few minutes! All I wanted was to be free!"

Her mum took her home that afternoon.

"Maybe there's another way," Mum murmured as they sat together on the sofa. Mum stroked her head. They listened to the birds singing outside.

Mina thought of telling her mum exactly what she'd done. She knew her mum would understand, or would be able to imagine. But she knew that what she'd done was very scary. And she didn't want to frighten her mum, to make her think that Mina would do something so dangerous.

Afterwards, Mina tried to think of ways to tell the tale. Then she thought that maybe it'd be best to write it down, which is what she did.

EXTRAORDINARY ACTIVITY
(THIRD-PERSON VERSION)
Write a story about yourself as if you're writing about somebody else.
(FIRST-PERSON VERSION)
Write a story about somebody else as if you're writing about yourself.

Did I really believe that the tunnel would lead to the Underworld? Did I really think that I could bring Dad home again? I'm the one who did it and even I don't know. I was a little girl. Awful things had happened and I was confused. Sometimes I wish I could go back there as if I was a big sister, and hug myself and say, "Don't worry, Mina. I promise that things will get better and you will feel stronger."

The tunnel still hasn't been opened to the public. Mum said that they discovered it would cost a fortune to make it safe. In places the tunnel had collapsed into unknown caverns. There were side tunnels that ended in rock falls or seemed to go nowhere. I never tried to go back again, of course. I never found out who the shadow in the shape of a man was, or what the dog was. I tried to tell myself that they were just part of the team trying to fix up the tunnel. But why would there be a dog? I tried to think that maybe it was just an ordinary man walking an ordinary dog and they'd gone into the tunnel just to see what it was like. But that seemed pretty unlikely. They haunted my dreams for weeks afterward. I still look out for them whenever we go to the park. Sometimes I think that Heston, the place where we live, is like ancient Greece, and that the Underworld is in the earth beneath us. I think of the King of the Underworld, Pluto, sitting on his throne deep down below. I think of his queen, the kind Persephone. Sometimes I think that I really did see something down there, something deep and ancient, and I wonder what would have happened if I'd kept on going, if I'd crossed the stream, if I'd walked toward the shadow in the shape of a man, if I'd said,

"My name is Mina McKee and I'm searching for my dad."

The best thing to come out of it all is the cat. I see him everywhere. His fur is even blacker than my hair. I call him Whisper. He is lovely. He is Whisper.

THOUGHTS ABOUT THE

ARCHAEOPTERYX

Ever since I made that model of the archaeopteryx, I've been holding it and swinging it through the air like it's flying. And I think about how it was the dinosaur that survived the disaster that wiped out all the other dinosaurs. And it didn't just survive. It evolved and became more elegant and skillful and powerful. It started the line of evolution that led to birds! And I look how the birds fly and soar over everything. I think of how they manage to inhabit the whole world, from the frozen poles to the steamy equator. And I've been thinking: if the human race manages to destroy itself, as it often seems to want to do, or if some great disaster comes, as it did for the dinosaurs, then the birds will still manage to survive. When our gardens and fields and farms and woods have turned wild, when the park at the end of Falconer Road has turned into a wilderness, when our cities are in ruins, the birds will go on flying and singing and making their nests and laying their eggs and raising their young. It could be that the birds will exist forever and forever until the earth itself comes to an end, no matter what might happen to the other creatures. They'll sing until the end of time. So here's my thought: If there is a God, could it be that he's chosen the birds to speak for him? Could it be true?

THE VOICE OF GOD SPEAKS THROUGH THE BEAKS OF BIRDS

ERNIE

MYERS,

RUBBISH,

DUST,

METEMPSYCHOSIS &
A BLUE CAR

I'm in the tree again. The buds of the leaves open more each day. The light that falls on me is dappled, and has a greenish tinge to it. The sky beyond is very blue. The blackbirds are very quiet. I wonder if the eggs are laid. I start to climb but the male bird suddenly flaps in the top branches and squawks and squawks.

"OK," I whisper. "I'll stay still."

I used to write on this tree, like it was some kind of secret notebook. I used to carve the letters into the bark with a little penknife and make sure that they couldn't be seen from below. Then I decided it was wrong to deface a wonderful thing like a tree, so I stopped. But I can still see them and touch them. My name, "Mina" (many times), and "Mum" and "Dad" (many times). "I hate EVERYTHING!" is carved onto one branch. "I LOVE everything!" is on another. "The World Is a Place of Wonder" is in elegant letters high up on the trunk. "Mina is lonely" is on a narrow branch, in very very tiny writing. The words are healing over now as time passes and the spring comes back. In a few years' time they won't be able to be seen at all.

I used to write on my arms as well, but I stopped that, too, except when I want to make a quick note to myself about something I've seen or heard.

Looks like they've finished clearing out Mr. Myers's house. The last of the junk's been carried out. There's been rubbish heaped up in the front garden for the last few days – broken furniture, boxes of old clothes, crockery, cutlery, ancient books and magazines. I see people pausing there. A couple of them have sifted through it all to see if there's anything of value or use. But there seems to be nothing. They throw it all back, take nothing away.

It's already been put up for sale. There's already been people eyeing it up. A man stared through the front window. He looked up at the roof. He scribbled notes in a notebook. Then a woman and a man climbed over the junk and stared into the front window. They turned and looked along the street as if they were inspecting it, checking whether it was up to their standard. They didn't see me. They looked very dull, very boring. "Don't you buy it!" I said inside myself. They said a few words to each other, then they shook their heads and walked away without a backward look.

"Good riddance!" I said inside myself.

Then a huge refuse wagon drove into the street. It stopped outside Mr. Myers's house with a great sighing of brakes. A man jumped down from the cab. He was dressed in orange overalls. He pulled on a pair of gloves and put a mask across his mouth, like he was dealing with something lethal. He lifted all the rubbish and threw it into the back of the wagon. He saw me watching. He laughed and waved. As he passed by my tree, he slowed right down and wound his window down.

"Hello, young'n!" he called.

His eyes were merry and bright.

"Hello," I answered.

"Looks like you're having a grand time up there in your tree!"

"I am," I said.

"Good lass!" He grinned, and shrugged, like he wanted to say something but didn't know what to say. Then he just called out, "Live your life, young'n!"

And he was gone, carrying the remnants of

Mr. Myers's life to the town dump.

What else can I do but live my life? But of course he meant, Live it well. Live it to the full. Which is a very nice thing to say to anybody, and which is exactly what I intend to do!

Suddenly the street was quiet and empty. I jumped down from the tree and went to Mr. Myers's house. I went to the front window, cupped my hands against the glass and peered inside. There was nothing, just dirty floorboards and lots of dust and beige wallpaper with faded flowers on it peeling from the walls. The ceiling was damp and cracked and a whole section of it had broken away. The door to the room was ajar. I imagined Mr. Myers shuffling through it with his zimmer frame into the corridor beyond. Mum had told me he'd been living downstairs for months. There was a bed and a toilet in what used to be the dining room.

Funny how somebody can just disappear from the world. Mr. Myers used to be a runner and a long jumper. He even had trials for England. He flew fighter planes in World War 2. He was married three times, Mum had told me. And now it was all over. But it wasn't, really, and he hasn't completely disappeared. Some of Ernie Myers must remain inside the house — flakes of his skin, for instance.*

* Extraordinary fact! Dust in houses (and in offices and schools and other places where humans live and work) consists mainly of tiny fragments of human skin. So when we see dust dancing and whirling and sparkling in a shaft of sunlight the thing that is dancing and whirling and sparkling is dead human skin! There's other stuff in there as well — like pollen and fibers of paper and cloth and flakes of the skin and hair of animals like cats, but the bulk of it is human skin! And lots of people's skin mingles together and dances in the light, and the skin of the living and the skin of the dead mingle together and dance in the light! And the skin of animals and the skin of humans mingle together and dance in the light! And this mingling is all around us, and is very ordinary and is very extraordinary and very strange!

EXTRAORDINARY ACTIVITY
Stare at Dust that Dances in the Light

And his smell must remain as well. And maybe they were the stains of his pee on the floorboards. Maybe there were molecules of Mr. Myers's breath still mingling with the air inside the house. Maybe his soul was still inside the house.

In some places, people believe that a person's soul stays near their home for many days after death before it flies away. In some places people believe that the soul never leaves this world, but takes the form of a bird. Imagine if that were true - that the birds we see around us are people's souls. I looked up to the roof, where a blackbird was calling. I held my hands against the brightness of the sky. Much higher up, I saw the tiny black dots of distant singing larks.

Then Mum was there, behind me. She put her hand on my shoulder.

"Wish I'd known him when he was young," I said.

Mum laughed.

"If you had, you'd be well on the way to being an old woman yourself." I pondered that fact. "He was a nice bloke," Mum said. "I always remember pushing you along in the buggy and he opened the door and came out. He put a pound coin into your hand. A bit of treasure for the baby, he said."

"Was Dad there?"

"Yes. Yes, he was." Then Mum flinched. "What's that?" she said.

"What's what?"

"That. Inside the house, Mina."

We both peered in through our hands, and we saw the black cat slinking out of the room through the open door.

"Oh," she breathed. "It's just a cat."

I smiled at the image of my little savage friend. I was certain there'd be mice aplenty for him in Mr. Myers's empty house.

"There's been people looking at the house already," I said.

"Good. Be nice to have new neighbors soon."

"But they might be boring," I said. "They looked very boring."

"You know you can't tell what somebody's like just by looking at them, Mina."

"Yes, I know that. But they did look boring, and ..."

She laughed.

"Maybe you should put a notice on the door. Only interesting people are allowed to buy this house!"

"Maybe I should."

"Anyway, buying a house is very complicated, and whoever buys this one will need to do lots of work, and that'll put people off, so just because somebody's looking at it doesn't mean anything."

"I know."

A blue car drove slowly past. The man driving it peered out. He stopped the car. The woman beside him leaned right down so she could see it too. She soon sat up again. They said a few words, he drove away.

"Be nice if a family bought it, wouldn't it?" said Mum.

I shrugged.

"Be nice if they had somebody round about your age, wouldn't it?"

"Don't care," I said.

She smiled gently.

"Don't you?"

"No. Just as long as they're ..."

"Interesting?"

"Yes! Interesting!"

She smiled again and I suddenly felt really awkward. She reached out and patted my arm.

"I'm sure they will be," she said.

We walked back home. The blue car drove into the street again and went slowly past the house again.

The blackbird squawked a warning call.

"Do you believe that birds are souls?" I asked.

She pondered.

"No. Not really. It's a nice thought, though. Do you?"

"No. Birds are quite extraordinary enough without having to be souls as well."

Mum went back into the house. I climbed back into the tree.

The blackbird watched me. I watched the man and the woman get out of the blue car. They

went to Mr. Myers's window. The woman appeared
to be pregnant. They looked very nice.

"Are the eggs here yet?" I whispered to the
blackbirds.

Squawk!

Squawk!

Squawk!

We had a lunch of cheese, bananas, iced buns,
and pomegranate juice. POMEGRANATE! YUM!
WHAT A TASTE! AND WHAT A WORD!

POMEGRANATE!

As we ate, Mum talked about birds and souls. She
said that some people believe the soul never dies, but
it moves from one body to another, even to the
bodies of animals. This is called the transmigration
of souls. It's a kind of rebirth, or reincarnation. She

talked about Plato and Hinduism and Buddhism. She said that some people believe that if you have not lived well you will be reborn as an insect, or even as a vegetable.

"Or as a fruit?" I said, holding up my banana.

"Yes, some people believe you could be reborn as a banana. Or as a pea, or a Brussels sprout."

I bit the banana.

"I wouldn't like to be a sprout. But a banana! Imagine being such a color and having such a taste!"

I bit the banana again. If there was a soul inside it, would you taste it? Or was the soul's taste the essence of banana-ness?

"Maybe good souls turn out bright and tasty," I said. "And bad souls turn out being green and yuck!"

"Maybe. Then raspberries, for instance, must be very good souls. And if you became an insect, what would a good soul be?"

"A dragonfly," I said. "Imagine being able

to do what a dragonfly does and to look like a dragonfly looks."

"Or a good soul could turn out to be a bee."

"To be a bee," I said. "To be a bee!"

"And a bad soul?"

"A cockroach."

"A bluebottle."

I pondered.

"I'd quite like to be a bird," I said.

"I can imagine you as a bird."

"A skylark, flying so high it can't be seen. Or a cat, as black as the night."

We were quiet for a time. We got on with our lunch. I tried to imagine what Dad might like to be, and I came up with a horse, a beast that's strong and fast and beautiful and proud. I didn't want to imagine him as another human being. The only human being I wanted him to be was my dad, even if he was just a memory of my dad.

"Another word for transmigration," said Mum, "is metempsychosis. It's a word from ancient Greece."

"Say it again."

"Met-em-sy-co-sis," she said, more slowly.

"Me-tem-sy-co-sis!" I said. "What a fantastic word! Metempsychosis! Metempsychosis! Met-em-sy-beautiful-co-sis!"

It is a great word! Look at it! Listen to it!

METEMPSYCHOSIS!
METEMPSY — BEAUTIFUL — CHOSIS

Then we looked at books about India and Sri Lanka, and read about Hinduism and Buddhism. We looked at photographs of the Himalayas, and I painted a picture of snow-capped mountains while Mum read to me about Tibet, the country beyond India high up in the clouds. In Tibet, people believe that the soul breaks free of the body at night, and has journeys that are remembered as dreams. This is known as astral traveling. Astral traveling! Imagine flying through the night with the bats and the owls, looking down at the house, the street, the city, the world!

They also believe that the whole of the universe hatched from a single egg. This makes total sense to me. Why shouldn't the universe have hatched from one of the most astonishing weird magical objects in the universe? An egg. A single egg! And if that is somehow true, then the whole universe is like a bird, flying through time. And each time it lays an egg itself, a whole new universe is created. And so there is universe after universe – a flock of universes flying through time.

A WISH & A PRAYER

IF MY SOUL, WHEN I DIE,
IS TAKEN BY THE BODY OF A BEAST,
I PRAY THAT THE BEAST WILL BE A BIRD,
AND THAT MY SOUL WILL BE UPLIFTED
BY THE BODY OF A LARK.

SPROUTS,
SARCASM &
THE MYSTERIES
OF TIME

I love afternoons like that, like when we talk about things like metempsychosis, when we learn so much, and wonder so much, and explore so much, and ideas grow and take flight, like the idea about the universe and the egg. I love being homeschooled, when we don't have to stick to subjects and timetables and rules. We've been doing it for nearly a year now, ever since the dreaded SATS Day. It seems much longer - maybe because it feels like we've got so much freedom and so much space and time. And we're very happy with it. Mum says it can't last forever, though. She says I'll become too isolated, especially as I'm an only child. She even says that schools aren't really prisons and cages. Yes, they bloody are! I tell her. She shakes her head and grins. Language! she says.

I love being on my own and with her (and with Whisper the cat and with the blackbirds and the owls). She knows that, and she says I'm coping very well, but just the other day she sat me down beside her and said,

"There'll come a time when you'll need more than this."

"No, I won't."

"Yes, you will. You'll need some friends, for instance."

"Friends?" I whispered.

She stroked my hair. She cuddled me, like I was tiny again.

"Yes, Mina. Friends. You'll have some lovely friends once you get started. And one day soon, of course, you'll even start thinking about boys."

"Thinking about what?"

"About boys."

I sniffed and looked away, even though I knew it was true.

"No I bloody well won't!" I said.

She laughed.

"Language! But don't worry. We'll take things slowly, step by step."

Is it true? Will I need to go to school again? I can't imagine it. Mum says I'm too extreme, but in my view schools are prisons and always have been and always will be. Here's a poem. I wrote it a couple of years back. I'll paste it into my journal now.

CONCRETE POEM TO EXPLAIN
THE MEANING OF
PAST PRESENT AND FUTURE
I HATED SCHOOL I HATED SCHOOL

I HATE SCHOOL I HATE SCHOOL

I WILL HATE SCHOOL I WILL HATE SCHOOL!

I HATED SCHOOL I HATED SCHOOL

I HATE SCHOOL I HATE SCHOOL

I WILL HATE SCHOOL I WILL HATE SCHOOL!

I HATED SCHOOL I HATED SCHOOL

I HATE SCHOOL I HATE SCHOOL

I WILL HATE SCHOOL I WILL HATE SCHOOL!

I HATED SCHOOL I HATED SCHOOL

I HATE SCHOOL I HATE SCHOOL

I WILL HATE SCHOOL I WILL HATE SCHOOL!

I HATED SCHOOL I HATED SCHOOL

I HATE SCHOOL I HATE SCHOOL

I WILL HATE SCHOOL I WILL HATE SCHOOL!

SEE HOW THE WORD
SCHOOL
LOSES ITS MEANING
THE MORE YOU REPEAT IT
JUST LIKE IT LOSES ITS MEANING
THE MORE YOU
ATTEND IT!

I wrote the poem after stupid Mrs. Scullery (or Sculley or whatever her name was) was trying to teach us about tenses, and about the differences between the present and the past and the future.

"Now listen carefully, children," she said, like we were slow and stupid or really young or something. "If I do something in the present I say I do it. If I say I did it in the past I say I did it. If I say I will do it in the future I say I will do it. Verbs are doing words*, and they have tenses — past tense, present tense and future tense. I have prepared an exercise for you. You must change the tenses of the. verbs as indicated. You understand? Of course you do. It is very plain."

And she handed some worksheets out. They contained a very boring story about a girl walking through a town and meeting lots of people along the way. Yawn, yawn. We had to change the present tense into the past. We got lots of sheets like that

*And incidentally VERBS ARE NOT "DOING WORDS." "Stop" is a verb. And if I say "I stop," I have stopped doing anything. I am doing absolutely nothing whatsoever at all! I would have told Mrs. Scullery that, but by this time she was getting totally fed up with me. She would have said, "That is just playing with words," and I would have answered, "And what is wrong with playing with words? Words love to be played with, just like children or kittens do!" Which she wouldn't have understood at all and which would have made her even more and more fed up.

from Mrs. Scullery — sentences with gaps where we had to stick in the missing words, or sentences with the words all mixed up and we had to unmix them to get them to make sense. They were all dead easy and all dead stupid. Usually I'd just put up with it and get on with it, but that day I must have clicked my tongue or something.

"Yes, Mina?" said Mrs. Scullery. "You have something to say?"

Usually I'd just say, No, Miss, but on that day I said, "The thing is, Mrs. Scullery, that it really isn't very plain at all. The past and the present and the future are much more mysterious than you say they are."

"Oh, are they? Then please do enlighten us."

That was so typical of her. SARCASM! I HATE SARCASM! Especially the kind that's done by teachers.

If I had anything to do with the running of schools, I'd have a big notice put into every single classroom:

SARCASM IS ABSOLUTELY FORBIDDEN!

I'd have another sign that said:

PLAYING WITH WORDS IS ABSOLUTELY ALLOWED!

Anyway, I did enlighten her.

"Yes, Miss," I said. "They are much much more mysterious. The past, for instance, was present to the people who lived in it. And the future will quickly become the present and will just as quickly become the past. And in our thoughts, the past and the present and the anticipation of the future exist together." She stood with her arms folded, waiting for me to go on. So I went on. "Right from the beginning of time, people have attempted to understand time, and they have not managed yet."

She sighed.

"Finished yet?" she said.

"No. So the mysteries of time cannot be reduced to a worksheet about tenses."

She sighed more deeply. She stared out of the classroom window into the darkening afternoon. I could see she was thinking that it would have been better for her to be something like a traffic warden or a police constable. Or a sprout, maybe.

"And that's to say nothing of our dreams," I said.

"Now you are finished. So please shut up! We are not doing Philosophy, Miss. McKee. This is an English lesson. So do your work!"

I did my work. I seethed inside. What about the dead? I wanted to ask her. They're supposed to be in the past but what if they're around us still (even as flakes of dust, for instance, to say nothing of souls)? Are we present when we're alive and past when we're dead? And what about the notion that we will rise again? What does that say about the present and the past and the future being different things? The things that the Mrs. Scullerys of the world take for granted and that they think are so plain are not plain.

I scribbled my stupid worksheet. Scullery sat at the desk and dreamed about being a sprout. I grabbed a piece of clean paper and started composing my concrete poem.

That day was near the end of my school days. Not much longer to go till I was at home with Mum. Before that, though, there'd be SATS Day. O my God, SATS Day! That's another of the tales I'll have to write. Then there'd be the day at the Corinthian Avenue Pupil Referral Unit. Now that's a day to write about.

EXTRAORDINARY ACTIVITY

Write a poem that repeats a word and repeats a word and repeats a word and repeats a word
until it almost loses its meaning.
(It can be useful to choose a word that you don't like, or that scares or disturbs you.)

Even though I hate school, I sometimes think it'd be very interesting to work in one. Or even to run one. I'd make sure there were some really interesting lessons, though I wouldn't call them "lessons." That's what my "Extraordinary Activities" are - much more exciting and productive than the worksheets put out by the Mrs. Scullerys of this world!

Here is another. I expect I will put in others as I go along.

EXTRAORDINARY ACTIVITY
(DAYTIME VERSION)

Touch the tip of the index finger to the tip of the thumb, making a ring. Look through the ring into the sky.* See the great emptiness there. Contemplate this emptiness. Wait. Don't move. Perhaps there is a tiny dot in the emptiness, which is a skylark singing so high up that it's almost out of sight. Perhaps not. Perhaps there really is just emptiness. Sooner or later a bird will appear for a second in your view and will fly away. Something appears in nothing, and then disappears. Keep looking. Sooner or later another bird will appear to take its place. Keep looking. It may be that several birds appear together. Keep looking. Keep looking. Allow the extraordinary sky into your mind. Consider the fact that your head is large enough to contain the sky. That is all, and it is hardly anything at all. No need to write anything down unless you would like to. Just remember. And wonder. And do the activity again when you have a moment. Do not worry about staring into space. It is an excellent thing to do.

*Do not look into the sun, of course. (Health & Safety Warning!)

EXTRAORDINARY ACTIVITY
(NIGHTTIME VERSION)

Touch the tip of the index finger to the tip of the thumb, making a ring. Look through the ring into the sky.* See the great abundance there. Contemplate this abundance: the stars and galaxies, the planets, the great great darkness, the stars so far away in time and space they look like scatterings of silver dust. Consider the unimaginable amount of space and time that is circled by the ring you have made. Consider that this unimaginable amount is just a tiny fragment of the universe, of eternity. Keep looking. Keep looking. Things will move across your vision: a flickering bat, a swooping owl; the high-up light of an airplane, the slow slow flashing of a satellite. Keep looking. Keep looking. Allow the abundant night into your mind. Consider the fact that your head is large enough to contain the night. That is all, and it is hardly anything at all. No need to write anything down unless you would like to. Just remember. And wonder. And do the activity again when you have a moment. Do not worry about staring into the dark. It is an excellent thing to do.

*Do not look into the moon, of course. (Health & Sanity Warning!)

PERSEPHONE, DAFTNESS & ABSOLUTELY NOTHING

Night again. Spring is strange. The year's supposed to be moving towards summer, but sometimes it seems to be turning right back to winter again. The sky was the color of steel all day. There was frost in the morning and it stayed all day under the trees and on the shady side of the garden wall.

I went out and climbed into the tree but the bark was icy and the breeze was bitter and even with two fleeces on I was freezing cold. The blackbirds didn't seem to care. They went on flying in and out of the tree, singing and squawking. But what if this year the spring didn't come at all? What if something dreadful had happened to the seasons for some awful reason?

I jumped down to the ground. Not a soul to be seen. I knelt on the grass and banged the ground with my fist and said,

"Come on, Persephone! Don't give up, Persephone!"

Persephone, who I thought I might meet during my journey to the Underworld, spends the winter in Hades with Pluto, the King of the Underworld. When it's time for spring she makes her way back up to the earth again. Spring doesn't start until she's back. In ancient Greece, they had music and dancing and singing to call her back, to make sure that spring arrived again.

"Come on!" I said, more loudly. I punched the ground again. I imagined her coming up through the earth's endless complicated tunnels. "Keep going! Don't get lost! Don't give up!"

I looked up and there was a woman, staring down at me. I think I recognized her from somewhere nearby. She had a checked green coat on, a woolly scarf, a yellow hat, white hair, and very kind eyes. She had a shopping bag on wheels with her.

"Are you all right, my dear?" she said.

"Yes, thank you."

"You'll catch your death down there," she said.

"I'll be all right. I'm just calling for Persephone."

She made a little laughing sound.

"The goddess of the spring!" she said.

"You know about her!"

"Of course I do, dear. Doesn't everybody?" She cupped a shaky hand around her mouth and whispered, "Come on, Persephone! Come back up to the world again! We're freezing cold up here!" She giggled. She looked around. "Folk'll think we're daft." She looked at me. "Do you think we're daft?"

"Yes," I said.

"Good. What's a world without daftness in it?"

WHAT'S A WORLD WITHOUT DAFTNESS IN IT? MY FEELING EXACTLY!

"What's your name?" she said.

"My name's Mina."

"Hello, Mina. My name's Grace."

"Hello, Grace."

She smiled and reached across the garden wall and took my hands in hers. Her hands were bony, dry and cold.

She winked at me.

"I've seen you in your tree, Mina. You look quite at home up there."

"I am."

"I used to love climbing, when I was a girl. I used to dream of climbing trees all day, stepping and swinging from one to the next, never once coming down to ground."

"Did you ever do it?"

"Not enough trees, Mina. But I made a lovely little circuit in my garden. From the corner of the outhouse, onto the apple tree, onto the top of a wobbly stepladder, then back to the outhouse again." She lifted her foot and giggled and groaned. "And these days I can hardly get up the blooming stairs."

An icy gust of wind blew along the street. She winced.

"Sometimes you look sad up there in your tree," she said.

"Do I?"

"Yes. But sad's all right. Sad's just part of everything."

She winked.

"Persephone!" she hissed. "Come on!" She said it again as if she was singing a little song, and I joined in with her.

"Come on, Persephone!

Come on, Persephone!"

She moved her hips like she was dancing and I joined in with her. She groaned softly and gritted her teeth and closed her eyes. Then she grinned.

"Bad bones," she said. "But never mind. They'll be fixed up soon and then ..."

Suddenly she put her hand to her mouth.

"Goodness gracious!" she said.

"What is it?"

"I just remembered, all of a sudden. I dreamed about you last night."

"About me?"

She laughed.

"Yes. You were in your tree and you said, Come on up here, Grace! So I climbed up beside you. You had tiny little feathers on you, just like a baby bird. Like a fledgling! Goodness gracious, we both did!"

She laughed again.

"That was all. I think."

I smiled back at her. It was lovely to think of being in Grace's dream.

"Isn't it funny," she said. "I'd forgotten all about it, and suddenly it all flooded back. Ah, well. That's how dreams go."

She squeezed my hands again. She took a deep breath and winced.

"She will come back again, Mina," she said. "She always does."

She tugged her scarf tighter on her throat.

"Got to keep moving," she said. "Bye-bye, Mina." She winked. "Maybe I'll dream about you again, eh?"

"That would be nice. Bye-bye, Grace."

She hesitated before she turned away

"Remember — she wants to be with us as much as we want to be with her. Keep calling her."

"I will."

She left the street. I thought about being in her dream. It was very strange. Maybe we're all in somebody's dream. Maybe everything's a dream, and nothing else.

I thought about that for a while, then I looked down at the ground again. I stamped on the ground.

"Persephone!" I hissed. "Come on back, Persephone!"

Then a loud banging noise started. I looked up and there was a man standing on the wall at Mr. Myers's house. He had a massive hammer in his hand and he was thumping a post down into the garden.

Thump! he went. Wallop! Thump! Smash!

Excellent, I thought. Persephone's bound to hear that. Thump it harder, mister.

He must have heard me. He thumped again.

WHACK! THUMP! WALLOP! SMASH!
COME BACK, PERSEPHONE!
WHACK! THUMP! WALLOP! SMASH!
COME BACK UP TO THE WORLD!

Then he gripped the post and shook it. Steady as a rock...

He nailed a sign to it:

FOR SALE
Stone & Co
Estate Agents

He jumped down and stamped the ground hard around the foot of the post. Then he briskly rubbed his hands together and grinned and walked away.

I punched the earth one more time, I stamped one more time.

"Come on, Persephone!" I said.

I imagined her, working her way past fossils and the remains of ancient cities. I looked up at the steel-gray sky. Not a chink of sunlight. I looked down again.

"Pay attention, please!" I said to her. "The world is in need of you!"

Then I came inside.

Mum was busy, writing an article for a magazine. That's what she does, articles for newspapers and magazines. She's even written about me sometimes, and about homeschooling. She says there are many good things about schools (which I do not agree with, of course!) but she also says that some schools, like some people, simply don't understand some simple facts about children.

SIMPLE FACTS ABOUT CHILDREN

CHILDREN HAVE TO BE LEFT ALONE SOMETIMES!
THERE'S NO NEED TO BE AT
THEM ALL THE TIME!
THERE'S NO NEED TO KEEP WATCHING THEM,
CHECKING THEM,
CRAMMING STUFF INTO THEM,
YANKING STUFF OUT OF THEM!
THERE'S NO NEED TO KEEP ON SAYING:

LEARN THIS, LEARN THAT!
DO THIS, DO THAT!
ANSWER THIS, ANSWER THAT!

SOMETIMES CHILDREN MUST BE
LEFT ALONE TO BE STILL AND SILENT,
AND TO DO

ABSOLUTELY NOTHING

AND SHE'S

ABSOLUTELY RIGHT!

WHY ARE WE SO SCARED OF
NOTHINGNESS? SHE ASKED.
GOOD QUESTION! WHY?
WHY ARE WE SO SCARED OF
NOTHINGNESS?
HERE IS A PAGE OF NOTHINGNESS.

IS IT SCARY? IS IT?

OF COURSE IT IS NOT!

EXTRAORDINARY ACTIVITY
Write an empty page. This is quite easy. Now look closely at the emptiness. This is quite easy, too, and quite delightful.

FIG ROLLS, PEE, SPIT, SWEAT & ALL THE WORDS FOR JOY

Mooched about. Had chocolate milk and two biscuits.

FIG ROLLS! DELICIOUS! SHOUT IT OUT! FIG ROLLS! DELICIOUS!

I know that some people do not like fig rolls — Sophie Smith, for instance. She was a girl at school that I sat next to for a while. She was almost as small as me. She had curly blond hair and blue eyes and she walked with a limp. I offered her a fig roll one breaktime.

"No thank you," she said. "I find them rather sickly."

"Sickly?" I said. "Rather sickly?"

I couldn't believe it.

"You must be joking!" I said.

"No," answered Sophie. "I prefer Jammy Dodgers."

I had to admit I'd never tasted a Jammy Dodger.

"What?" she said. "Never tasted a Jammy Dodger? Where on earth have you been all your life?"

Next day she brought some Jammy Dodgers into school. She gave me one at break.

"Well?" she said.

"Delicious!" I said, so she gave me another.

We were friends for a while, I suppose. We used to walk around the yard at breaktimes. One day I took a deep breath and said,

"I know it's nothing to do with me, but why do you limp?"

"I had a disease when I was little," she said. "It left a problem with my leg."

"That's a shame."

"Does it worry you?" she said.

"No," I answered. "Of course it doesn't."

We walked on.

"I'll have an operation to sort it out when I'm a bit older," she said.

"That's good."

"It'll mean some pain, but I think it'll be worth it."

Then she looked at me and said,

"Can I ask you something?"

"I suppose so."

"Why are you so ...?"

She stopped.

"So what?" I said.

She shrugged.

"So strange, I suppose," she said.

"Am I?"

"Kind of. A bit kind of complicated."

I looked at the kids in the yard, running round together, hanging out together.

"I don't mean to be," I said. I laughed. "Maybe I should have an operation to fix it."

She laughed as well.

"Maybe you should. But what kind of operation would fix strangeness?" she said.

"I have no idea," I said.

"A destrangification operation!" she said.

We laughed together at the word.

"Does it worry you?" I said.

"No," she said.

She reached into her pocket and brought out a package wrapped in silver foil.

"Have a Jammy Dodger," she said.

I grinned.

"Delicious!"

Sophie Smith. I wonder where she is now. In the same school? Has she moved away? Does she like fig rolls at last? Has she had her operation? Probably I'll never find out. I did think I saw her passing by the end of the street one day, while I was sitting in my tree, but I wasn't certain. I almost called out to her, but I didn't. Would I like to see her again? Yes, I suppose I would.

I would only ever whisper it, but I do sometimes think I will have to go back to school one day, and make some new friends. Sometimes I would quite like to go back. And I should also whisper that all of the teachers weren't Mrs. Scullerys. Some were nice, and interesting, and creative. Like Mr. Henderson, who told us about the tunnels under Heston Park. And like some other teachers I had in the past. And there were nice kids like Sophie. Sometimes I find myself thinking that a school could be (could be!) a wonderful place. Sometimes I even find myself thinking that there already are schools that are wonderful places. But that makes no real difference. Schools are still

CAGES and PLACES TO BE AVOIDED!

FIG ROLLS! WOW! I like to nibble the top of the biscuit off first, then chew away the lovely figgy stuff (it's lovely slooched around inside the mouth with chocolate milk), then eat the bottom bit.

Went up to the loo. Listened to the lovely tinkling sound of my pee splashing down into the water. Thought about water running through me, water and my pee being flushed away into the drains, how it'll end up in rivers and seas and how it'll evaporate into the air and come back down again as rain. Lovely to think of water that's been my pee coming down as rain! Maybe that's why people say it's pissing down!

Water's moving all the time, running, flowing, swirling, splashing, gurgling, evaporating, condensing. Some of the water molecules that are in me now were once in the Red Sea, or in the Mississippi, or in Ernie Myers, or in a blackbird, or in an orange, or a sprout, or inside a dinosaur, or in a caveman, or a saber-toothed tiger, or a three-toed sloth or ...

I spat down into the water and flushed

again and off went my spit into the world. It'll change from being spit. Some of it will turn up in somebody else and then in somebody else's spit and pee. It'll become a bit of the Pacific Ocean or the Nile. It'll turn up in whatever kind of beings we become in the future. And on and on and on and onto the very end of time.

EXTRAORDINARY ACTIVITY
Go to the loo. Flush your pee away.
Consider where it will go to and what it will become.

Swigged some water from the tap to replace the water I have lost through spit and pee and sweat. The human body is 65 percent water. Two-thirds of me is constantly disappearing, and constantly being replaced. So most of me is not me at all!

Gulp!

MOST OF ME IS NOT ME!
MOST OF MINA IS NOT MINA!
MOST OF ANYBODY IS NOT ANYBODY!

Caught sight of myself in the bathroom mirror. Stepped back and had a good look. I am indeed very skinny. This must be an organic thing, given my fondness for fig rolls and Jammy Dodgers and chocolate. And I'm rather small. When I was young Mum used to call me her little bird, which I loved. But however small and light I might be, I can't be as light as a bird is. They have air cavities within their bones. The correct word for this fact is pneumatization. Pneumatization. What a word! NEW-MA-TIZE-ATION.

PNEUMATIZATION!

I, along with all other human beings, am not pneumatized. Therefore I am earthbound. Or am I? Maybe not. After all —

**MY PEE AND MY SWEAT AND MY SPIT RISE INTO THE AIR
AS VAPOR AND FALL TO THE EARTH AS RAIN.
MY SKIN DANCES IN THE AIR AS DUST.
MY BREATH MERGES WITH THE AIR AND WITH THE SKY.
SO I AM EARTHBOUND BUT ALSO AIRBOUND!**

I keep on looking. I know that the girl I see in the
bathroom mirror will evolve and grow. Mum says I
am poised on the threshold of a time of wonder. I
look at the little creature in the mirror and it seems
impossible. But yes, I do feel poised. And I'm also
happy to wait, and to be a baby in those times I
need to be a baby, like when Mum wraps her arms
around me on the sofa and whispers that she loves
me, and sings her songs to me, and whispers that
I'm her lovely little chick.

Mooched about some more. Went to my bedroom
and mooched through my bookshelves. Pulled out
three books, three of the extraordinariest books in the
world: *Where the Wild Things Are*, *We're Going on
a Bear Hunt* and *Dogger!* Lay on my bed and read
them and looked at them just like I did when I
was a little girl. And danced the dance of the Wild
Things with Max, and tiptoed into the bear's cave
with the family, and felt really sad with Dave
about his lost toy, Dogger, and really happy with
him when he found it again.

I read them all again, a second time, and got all dreamy, and remembered Dad, the way he was when he used to read these books to me just before I went to sleep. I never really have a strong picture of him in my mind. I sort of half-hear him and half-see him, like he's somebody in a dream that gets harder to remember the more you try to think of him. When I read the words to myself I can kind of half-hear the sound of his voice as he read them to me.

I half-remembered the smell of his breath and the stubble on his cheek as he kissed me good night, the slight roughness of his skin as he stroked my cheek, his voice as he whispered his Good Night. And I lay with the books around me and the strange half-vague, half-intense memories* inside me, and felt very small indeed.

This activity has made me rather sad. I will cheer myself up by writing all the words for joy and loveliness, two whole pages filled with nothing else!

---

* A strange thought. Maybe trying to remember when you are young is very like trying to remember when you are old. When he looked out into the street, Ernie Myers probably felt like I did when I was trying to look back into the past. So the young and the old are in some ways very alike.

skylark Mum blackbird owl moon tree park
Icarus wing weird cat black shining silver
smooth joy yes egg tree nest light toast
marmalade raspberry yogurt park Mina
Dad bat Orpheus angel night whisper
journal Sendak book abundant story sing
dance Grace starling Mina mess clutter sing
beak God fly typical William joy pollen
nonsense sloth wild painter poet Blake
savage coal fig tender wander Rosen
wonder banana transmigration Hughes
flush unimaginable Dave paint clay dangle
alarm witch Buddhism saint skin weirdo
pebble crow pissing grandpa Oxenbury
Ernie heaven universe Max star Dogger
imagine tinkling alive glisten bud beat

beautiful inside soul tatty hatch chick wet

creature book lullaby Maurice sloosh light

water pizza love paradox alive hoot giggle

Hinduism darling purr lass zimmer

Persephone pee poo soul fig bloke strange

bee imagine Shirley chocolate goggly word

Grace metempsybeautifulchosis bony wallop

Himalaya cloud body hatch universe stupid

bloody archaeopteryx poem word yawn

nothingness mystery click tongue

mysterious sprout thump carrot philosophy

see pomegranate sweat Helen dead concrete

Corinthian stop play index finger biscuit

space saber madness spring Michael cheese

strange world winter frost extraordinary

earth this dream dust silver sleep o sun

When that was done, I looked out into the street. The blue car was back. The pregnant woman and the man got out. There was a boy with them. The woman looked at Mr. Myers's house with distaste, but the man guided her to the front window. They peered in. The boy stood with his hands in his pockets and stared glumly at the earth. He stared glumly along the street. The man grinned at him and called him forward. The boy didn't move. Then another car came, and a man in a suit, carrying a plastic folder, got out. He shook the hands of the woman and the man. The boy just looked away. The man in the suit laughed. He seemed to say something, probably something about "kids." He rubbed his hands and took some keys out of his pocket and opened the front door. They went inside.

I sat at the table. I doodled. Wrote some nonsense. Kept looking from the window. Saw Whisper slinking along by the low garden walls.

The family were inside the house for an age. I imagined them moving from room to room, moving through the molecules of Ernie Myers. I imagined them inspecting the collapsing ceilings, the toilet in the dining room, the dilapidated garage at the back.

"Don't be discouraged," I said inside myself. "We need things to be born around here!"

Then they came out again at last.

The two men shook hands. The man in the suit drove off. The other man grinned, and opened his arms wide as if he wanted to wrap the house in them. The woman brushed herself with her hands, trying to get rid of dust and dirt. The man whispered to her. He stroked her belly. They both held her belly. She laughed. The boy stared down at the earth. He kicked it hard. He scowled. He probably swore. He kicked the earth again. And again.

They went away. It was turning to dusk. There was much birdsong in the street.

I went downstairs.

"More visitors to Mr. Myers's house," I say.

"That's good," says Mum. "Boring visitors or interesting visitors?"

I shrugged.

"Don't know. They went in with the estate agent."

"Must be quite interested, then."

"The woman didn't look interested at all. Nor the boy."

"The boy?"

"Yes, Mum. The boy."

"Now that'd be nice."

"Would it? And the woman's going to have a baby."

"Now that definitely would be nice!"

She smiled and reached out and tousled my hair.

"Anyway, what have you been up to?"

"Talking to an old lady with bad bones, dancing for Persephone, being in somebody else's dream, thinking about pee and sweat and spit, reading Where the Wild Things Are and writing a thousand words for joy."

She laughed again.

"Sounds like a fine day's work to me."

**EXTRAORDINARY ACTIVITY
(JOYOUS VERSION)**
Write a page of words for joy.
**EXTRAORDINARY ACTIVITY
(SAD VERSION)**
Write a page of words for sadness.

GRANDPA, MISSING MONKEYS & OWLS

Now it's night. No stars. Mist is hanging in the street. Frost is glittering. "IT'S SUPPOSED TO BE SPRING!" I want to yell. "SO GET LOST, FROST!"

An owl hoots, from the direction of Mr. Myers's house. It hoots again, and something hoots in answer.

Owls. I feel so close to them. I share a home with them.

"Good night, owls," I whisper. "I'll write your story tomorrow."

Hoot.   Hoot   hoot   hoot.

MINA & THE OWLS

Mina's mother's father was a seaman. Ever since he was a young man, he had sailed the world. He had been everywhere, to so many exotic-sounding places with such exotic-sounding names: Santiago, San Francisco, Cairo, Casablanca, Java, Buenos Aires, Fiji, Honduras, Tokyo, Reykjavik, Manila, Singapore, Bangkok, Abu Dhabi, Hanoi ... The list could go on forever — or for as long as a list of exotic places could last.

Mina remembered getting postcards from those places when she was a tiny girl. Her grandpa traveled so much that Mina only met him a few times. She remembered a busy and funny man with a big laugh and skin the color of hazelnuts. She remembered his stories about the lions and tigers and crocodiles he's fought in distant jungles, the whales he'd swum with, the whirlpools he'd escaped from, the treasure he'd discovered in sunken galleons. He said he'd bring back a treasure chest for her one day. He said he'd bring her a monkey. Even then, she knew the tales and promises were made up. She knew, for instance, that lions don't live in jungles. But she did kind of hope that the tale about the monkey might come true!

He always said he'd stop traveling, that he'd retire and return to the house he had on Crow Road, but Mina's mum knew that he never would. He went on sailing long beyond the time he could have stopped. He ended up doing trips in little sailing boats for tourists in the Indian Ocean. In his last postcard, he said he would be back very soon. He also said that he was looking for the right kind of monkey. He also said that he was in Paradise.

When he died he was buried at sea, in the Indian Ocean at dusk.

In his will, he left everything to Mina's mum, but said the house on Crow Road should go to Mina when she became twenty-one. He said she was "the little girl that I have carried in my heart across the seven seas." Mina liked that thought, that while she was at home in Falconer Road, she was also traveling around the exotic places of the world.

Inside the will, there was a folded note with

her name written on it. It said:

P.S. Remember. It's just a house. Don't get stuck in it. Be free. Travel the world.

P.P.S. Sorry about the monkey!

P.P.P.S. Sorry we didn't get to see each other much.

P.P.P.P.S. Live your life.

P.P.P.P.P.S. The World is Paradise.

P.P.P.P.P.P.S. Sorry I died (which I must have done as you're reading this!).

P.P.P.P.P.P.P.S. Bye-bye. Lots of love, Grandpa.

Mina had hardly been in the house until then. It was a big three-story place on Crow Road near the park. Mum had been born in it, but had no memories of living in it. When she was three, her dad started his traveling, and she moved with her mum to a smaller house, and grew up there.

The big house was never sold. Mum said it was always there as a reminder that her dad might come back again and settle down, even though she and her mum knew in their hearts that he never would.

"Did Grandma keep on loving him?" Mina asked one day.

Mum shrugged and sighed. "She said she did. But it's hard to go on loving somebody that's always on the seven seas." She smiled. "Grandma was quite a force herself, of course." She winked. "She was liked by lots of men."

For a few years while Mina was growing up, the house was rented out to students. Mina remembered seeing them sometimes, going in and out of the house, rolling bicycles into the hallway, sitting in the front garden eating sandwiches, throwing Frisbees, playing guitars. She remembered wondering what it would be like, to live in a big house like that with lots of friends, and to throw Frisbees in the garden, though she found it hard to think of herself with lots of friends. Then she thought, Maybe I'll find friends who are rather like me, and we'll be able to put up with each other.

The students didn't last forever. The house was getting run-down. It needed decorating, some of the window frames were starting to rot, the electrics needed to be fixed up. Mina's mum wrote

to Grandpa about it. He said he'd sort it out soon.
They knew, of course, that he never would. So
Mina's mum locked the house, put boards across the
windows and put a sign on the door that simply
said:

DANGER

And for a long time, the house was almost
forgotten about.

One afternoon, just after the reading of the will,
Mum got the key to the house out of a drawer. She
found a torch. She and Mina put on old clothes, and
they walked to Crow Road, to the dark green gate
that led to the house. Mum unlocked the gate and
they walked through the garden to the DANGER
door. Mum unlocked that too. She pushed it open,
stepped aside and bowed.

"Welcome to your inheritance, Mistress
McKee," she said in a spooky-sounding voice, and
she ushered Mina into the inside darkness.

The house had big rooms, bare floorboards,

143

bare walls. Mum shone the torch up into the corners to show the heavy plasterwork, the wallpaper curling away from the walls, the dangling light fixtures. There were cobwebs everywhere. Little creatures kept scuttling across the floors. Chinks of light shone through the cracks in the boards on the windows. Dust (skin!) danced through the torch beam. They climbed the wide stairways. Their footsteps echoed and echoed through the house.

"What on earth will you be doing with something so large?" said Mum.

"I shall live in it with my servants, of course," said Mina. "Or I shall establish a school."

"A school, my lady?"

"Yes. A school for the writing of nonsense and the pursuit of extraordinary activities."

They climbed three stairways. On the final landing there was a final narrow flight of stairs.

Mum paused.

"This leads to the attic," she said. She shuddered. "I remember hardly anything of being in this house, but I do remember looking up these stairs and feeling very weird."

"Weird?" said Mina.

"Yes, scared, and ... weird."

"Let's go up," said Mina.

Mum held back.

"Do I dare?"

Mina led the way. The stairs were narrow. She reached towards the attic door and opened it.

They were in a wide room. Light came in from an arched window that had not been boarded. Beyond the window was the park, then the roofs and spires and towers of the city, and the wide wide sky. The window was broken. Glass lay on the floor beneath. There were large bird droppings upon the glass.

"Look!" said Mina.

In one of the walls there was a hole where plaster and bricks had fallen away. Below the hole there were more droppings, a few brown and black feathers and some furry balls. Mum held Mina back.

"A nest!" hissed Mina.

Slowly, slowly, she approached it.

"Mina, take care!" whispered her mother.

But Mina wasn't scared. The hole in the wall

was as high as her head. She stood on tiptoes and peered into the shadowed space. She saw the feathered bodies lying there together. She saw the bodies moving as the birds breathed.

"Oh, Mum! Oh, come and look!"

Her mum came close. She stood on tiptoes, too, and peered in.

"Owls!" whispered Mina. "Sleeping in the day, they must be owls."

They stared in wonder for a moment, then they backed away. Mum bent down and picked up two of the furry balls.

"Owl pellets," said Mum.

They crouched against the wall beside the door.

Mum tugged at one of the pellets and broke it apart. She showed fur and skin and tiny bones in her hand.

"They eat their victims whole," she said. "Whatever can't be digested is brought up and discarded."

She put the second pellet into Mina's hand. Mina held it. Once this furry lump had been a vole or a mouse. Mina watched the nest. She had a vision of the owls rising from their sleep, emerging from the wall, flying out into the city sky. She imagined them hunting in the park.

Outside it was still bright day.

"Mum," she said. "Let's stay till night. Let's see them fly."

Mum's eyes were glazed with the reflection of the sky as she looked back at her. She glanced at her watch. Dusk was an hour or more away. But Mina knew that her mum was as enchanted by the vision of the owls as she was herself.

"What if they attack us?" said Mum.

"We'll get prepared. We'll open the door. We'll lie on the stairs and get ready to close it again if they come for us."

And that's what they did. They lay on the stairs and they waited. The sky outside the window slowly darkened. They lay together and could feel each other's beating hearts.

"I don't know what to do," said Mum. "We should get the window fixed. It's letting in the damp."

"But the owls," said Mina.

"I know," said Mum. She shook her head. "What are they doing nesting in the house? They should be in the park, in a tree."

Mina smiled. It seemed so mysterious and so right. There were owls, creatures of dreams and the night, living in her house!

"I'm uncomfortable," said Mum. "My knees are getting sore. What kind of silly woman does a thing like this when there's so much that's sensible to be done?"

"A silly woman like you," said Mina. "It won't be long."

The shadows in the attic deepened. The sky outside turned orange, red, then inky blue, and then the silveriness of moonlight was in the sky. They lay dead still. They breathed more gently.

"They're birds of wisdom," whispered Mum. "They're the symbol of seeing hidden, secret things."

"So we should be pleased to have them in the house."

"Yes, we should be pleased."

They watched and watched, and then their

hearts began to thunder. There was movement in the nest, a rustling of feathers, a sudden low sharp screech.

And Mina and her mother gasped. A bird stood in the hole in the wall: dark feathers, shining eyes. They saw the head turning. Then another bird appeared. Mum held the edge of the door, ready to slam it shut. There was another low screech and then the birds leapt into the air, and seemed massive as they flew a circle around the room. They perched together on the sill for a moment in the moonlight, then they leapt again, and flew out into the night.

They rose to their feet. They gasped and giggled at the thrill of what they'd seen.

"Extraordinary," whispered Mina, and somewhere far away a hooting started.

Hoot. Hoot hoot hoot.

"We'll leave the window as it is," said Mum.

"No we won't," said Mina, and she lifted a piece of broken brick from the floor, went to the window and knocked away more of the glass above the sill, making the opening wider and safer for the birds. She gazed out. She imagined leaping, like the birds did, like Icarus did in the story from long ago. She imagined her wings spreading as she swooped over the city.

Then they left the attic. As they entered the stairwell, Mina felt a creature winding itself around her feet.

"Oh," she gasped, and then she smiled.

"Who's this?" said Mum.

"My familiar little friend," said Mina. "I've called him Whisper."

Later, in the house, at the kitchen table, Mina made models of the owls from heavy clay and laid them on the table. She opened up the owl pellet in a bowl of warm water. She loosened the scraps of skin and fur and bone. She laid the fragments of what had been a mouse or a vole on her table. It was still gorgeous, so mysterious. It had been alive, it had been killed by an owl, it had been inside the owl and now it was out again. It was in her fingers, on the palm of her hand, on her table beside a clay model of an owl. Later, in her dreams, she made owls as light as spirits, and she flew with them in the night.

OWL

YOU FLY IN THE VELVET NIGHT.
YOU SEE WHAT CAN'T BE SEEN,
YOU HEAR WHAT CAN'T BE HEARD.

LEND ME YOUR FEATHERS
AND BONES AND WINGS.
LEND ME YOUR EYES
AND EARS AND CLAWS.
LEND ME THE HEART
TO LEAP LIKE YOU
INTO THE ASTONISHING NIGHT.

SATS DAY, GLIBBERTYSNARK & CLAMINOSITY!

It was always writing that got me into trouble with Mrs. Scullery. She said I just EXASPERATED her.

"You could be one of my very best pupils, Mina McKee — one of the very best I have ever had, in fact. But you are a constant disappointment! You let the school down, you let your poor mother down, and most of all you let YOURSELF down, time and time and time again. You are a silly and wayward and undisciplined child. Instead of concentrating on the task in hand, you spend your time playing about and drawing attention to yourself and your silly foibles!"

Draw attention to myself? That was just about the last thing I wanted. I wanted to disappear. I didn't want to be there at all!

The day that brought it to a head was SATS day. SATS Day, the day she started out so calm and sweet, the day she ended screaming out loud in front of the whole class, the day she snarled that I was full of nothing but stupid crackpot notions, the day she put her hands on her hips, glared straight into my face and growled,

"Mina bloody McKee. You are full of sheer

bloody daftness and you are an utter bloody disgrace!"

Bloody. She said it in front of the whole class. It was unheard-of! A teacher said bloody in front of the whole class! That showed how bad things had become!

It was nonsense that did it. And it was SATS day! SATS day! Aaagh! Everybody just had to stay calm! It was nothing special! But everybody was so stressed out! Everybody was so scared! Everybody was so focused on making sure that the school was up to standard. Everybody was so concerned that everybody would all turn out to be better than the average of children of our age throughout the country! Everybody was so concerned that we would get Level 4 and Level 5 and Level 99! We shouldn't get worked up about it, though! We should just treat SATS day as another ordinary school day! It wasn't really a test at all! It was just a way of checking that things were going OK at St. Bede's! It wasn't really a test of the kids! It was a test of the school! So nothing to do with the kids at all! So just stay calm! So just don't worry! Just relax! JUST RELAX! SATS Day was just another ordinary day! But SATS Day was SATS Day! IT WAS SATS DAY!

ᴀᴀᴀᴀᴀᴀᴀGH!SATS DAY!

It started quietly enough. There we were sitting in class, some of the kids white-knuckled as they gripped the edge of their tables, some of them, such as Sophie, chewing their lips, some of them slouched and not caring at all. Some were poised and well prepared and smiling in anticipation, like Samantha, with new pens and pencils laid out neatly on the tables in front of them.

Mrs. Scullery looked like she'd spent the night seeing ghosts. Her hair was sticking out. Her lipstick was slashed across her chops. Her dress was buttoned up all wrong. Her hands were trembling. She goggled red-eyed from her desk at us.

"Remember," she said to us in a high-pitched wobbly voice. "You must simply do your best, children." She gave especially appealing glances to the ones she thought were cleverest, like me. "Just do your best. Please do your best. Please..."

I felt sorry for her. I really did. I felt that somebody should get up and go to her and give her a big hug and say,

"Don't worry, Mrs. Scullery. It will all be all right."

But nobody did.

Then she gave the papers out. We had to keep them facedown until she gave the word. Then she said it.

"Turn your papers over and you may begin."

Oh my God I couldn't stand it. Why should I write what they told me to write just because they told me to write it? What was the point of that? Why should I write because the school and everybody in it was so stupendously and stupidly stressed out? Why should I write something so somebody could say I was well below average, below average, average, above average or well above average? What's average? And what about the ones that find out they're well below average? What's the point of that and how's that going to make them feel for the rest of their lives? And did William Blake do writing tasks just because somebody else told him to? And what Level would he have got anyway?

"Little Lamb, Who mad'st thee? Dost thou know who mad'st thee?"

What Level is that? And what about Shakespeare? "Double, double, toil and trouble; Fire burn and cauldron bubble!" What Level's that? Would Shakespeare have been well above average? And Dickens and Chaucer and Keats and Shirley Hughes and Maurice Sendak and Michael Rosen? Did any of them do stupid silly SATS! I SUSPECT NOT!

I stared out the window for a while. There were no flies dancing in the air that day, though the sunlight was particularly beautiful where it shone on the drops of water left on the glass after a little rain shower. Maybe I'd be able to write about that, or about the birds that kept flitting back and forward. And there was a lovely pattern where the paint had flaked away at the edge of the window frame. Or maybe I could write a story about Mrs. Scullery's night with the ghosts. I heard my name whispered. Mina McKee. I looked up. Mrs. Scullery was glaring at me. Everybody was heads down getting their writing done. Mrs. Scullery whispered my name again. I looked at her. I nodded at her and sighed. Poor Mrs. Scullery. I read the first instruction on the paper. "Write a description of a busy place." Oh my God. I looked up again. THE HEAD TEACHER was looking in through the glass bit of the classroom door. He looked like he'd been with the ghosts as well. He looked like he was about to burst into tears. He caught my eye. He mouthed the words: WRITE. DON'T WORRY! PLEASE WRITE. The poor poor man. So I smiled at him, and nodded, and shrugged, and started to write, and this is what I wrote.

GLIBBERTYSNARK

In thi biginin glibbertysnark woz doon in the woositinimana. Golgy golgy golgy thang, wiss wandigle. Oliotoshin under smiffer yes! Glibbering mornikles which was o so diggibunish. Hoy it! Hoy it! Then woz won so stidderuppickle. Aye aye woz the replifing clud. Yes! Clud is cludderish thats trew. Tickles und ticklin woz the rest ov that neet dun thar in the dokniss; An the crippy cralies crippin unda the path doon thar. Howzit! Woz the yel. Howzit! Sumwun nose a sekritish thang an wil holed it unda. Aye! Unda! So hoy it! Naa. It is two riddish a thang for hoyin. So giv it not a thowt. Arl wil be in the wel in the wel ay depe don in the wel. An on it goze an on an on an on an on an on an on an on til the middlishniss is nere. An the glibbertysnark wil raze oot the woositinimana an to the blewniss wi the burds an clowds an clowds this loke lyke clowns. An wil laff laff laff. An wil yel Hoy it! Hoy it! Til the lasst ov the daze wen we wil no a ansa. So pond the glibbertysnark an the olitoshin an kip way ov mornikles. Yel howzit an hoy it! Til the bels is ringerish.

An rite words for scullery an hedteechery coz ov the gosts an goolys an the sats an orl wil be wel wel wel. In conclooshun woopwoopwoopiness is pringersticks wif strattikipiness coz the ansa iz hidin in the cludderish claminosity wer the clowdiwinkling quakilstrator iz. Luk no wer wer the blippistrakor ov munomintelish plirders iz. Ther: Is dun. Hoy it! Hoy it! Hoy it! Til the coos cum bak acros the flisterin feeld unda the mistrictacular moooooon. Flap! An ther rite now its endid. Pop!

RESULT:

Mrs. Scullery:	Not Pleased. The "Mina Bloody McKee Bloody Disgrace" Scene. (see above)
HEAD TEACHER:	Not Pleased. The "Who Do You Think You Are Madam I Am Calling Your Mother" Scene. (see below)
Grade Achieved	Level 0 Well Well Well Below Average.
Mum	Very Sad, Very Kind, Then Very Determined.
Mina	Created new words (Glibbertysnark! Oliotoshin! Claminosity! Blippistrakor!) Therefore: Very Pleased. TAKEN OUT OF SCHOOL! Therefore: VERY VERY VERY PLEASED.

I thought I had done very well in such a short time. They didn't even read it right through. Mrs. Scullery held it up like it was a poisonous thing. She did the "bloody" scene. She got to the bit where she said I was an utter bloody disgrace. Then she leaned right down so that her face was nearly right in mine. For a moment I wanted to stroke it. I wanted to give her a cuddle, I really did. She looked O so stressed out. I wanted to say, "O, Mrs. Scullery. Never mind. It's just some writing, that's all. It's not going to harm you. And look, some of it's lovely. Don't get yourself worked up, love. Calm down. I'm sure Samantha has done some lovely level 5ish work."

But I couldn't get any words out. I just stared back into her eyes.

"You," she whispered hard into my face. "You, madam."

"Me?" I whispered back.

"Are as hard as iron."

And she led me to THE HEAD TEACHER and gave the writing to him. He looked at it like it was another ghost come back to haunt him. He held

it up and twisted his face like it was a very very
dangerous stinking poisonous thing.

"What," he said, "is this?"

"Writing," I said.

"Writing what?"

"Writing, sir."

"And what kind of writing do you think it is?"

He glared. He fumed. He gritted his teeth.
Did he really want to know?

"It's nonsense, sir," I said.

"EXACTLY, MADAM. IT. IS.
NONSENSE! IT. IS. A PAGE. OF ABSOLUTE.
AND TOTAL. UTTER. IDIOTIC. NONSENSE!"

I could see he wanted to swear, just like
Mrs. Scullery had. I wanted to tell him it was OK
to tell me I was an utter bloody disgrace, if he
wanted to.* I wanted to tell him he could use even
worse words if it would help him feel better. I
wouldn't mind at all. But I thought it was
probably best not to say that.

"I know that, sir," I simply said.

---

* Thoughts about swearing. Yes, I know that swearing is very bad, and that swearwords
are very very bad bad things. But there are times when nothing else will work —
otherwise why have swearwords at all? And I know that you are not supposed to say this,
but there are times when swearwords just sound very nice and feel nice on your tongue
and are simply very nice to say. (I don't think Mrs. Scullery would agree with any of this,
despite her performance in the Bloody Disgrace scene.)

"Oh, you know that, do you? So who do you think you are? And what right do you have to ..."

"I don't know, sir. Sometimes I wonder, Who am I? What am I doing ..."

Mrs. Scullery groaned. She gripped the edge of THE HEAD TEACHER's desk.

"Are you taking the mick, young lady?" said THE HEAD TEACHER.

"No, sir."

Mrs. Scullery groaned again.

"Doreen!" yelled THE HEAD TEACHER.

Doreen came in from the room next door. Doreen was THE HEAD TEACHER's secretary.

"Yes, Headmaster?" said Doreen.

"I need this young lady's telephone number, please, Doreen."

I started to say that I knew it but he stopped me with a glare.

Doreen went out and came back again with the number.

"Thank you, Doreen," said THE HEAD TEACHER. "That will be all for now."

He lifted the telephone. He dialed the number.

166

He spoke to Mrs. McKee about her daughter. He said he would like to see her, now, if at all possible.

"No," he said. "She has not had an accident, Mrs. McKee, but I should like to see you in person if I may."

He put the phone down.

"She is on her way," he said.

"She won't be long," I started. "We just live—"

"We KNOW where you live!" said THE HEAD TEACHER. "We need no further contributions from you, thank you very much! Mrs. Scullery, would you like a glass of water? You look a little..."

"Oh yes, please, Headmaster. Thank you, Headmaster," said Mrs. Scullery.

"And do take a seat, Mrs. Scullery. Doreen! A glass of water for Mrs. Scullery, please."

Doreen brought the water in. They sat. I stood. We waited in silence. I stared at a painting on the wall. It showed a delicious-looking bowl of fruit. I imagined that on bad days (like today, perhaps) THE HEAD TEACHER gazed at this fruit and dreamed of what he could have been instead of A HEAD TEACHER. A banana, for instance. Or a plum. Or a bunch of grapes. I tried to imagine THE HEAD TEACHER as a bunch of grapes. He might be much happier that way.

Minutes passed. Mrs. McKee arrived and was brought into the room by Doreen.

"Thank you for coming, Mrs. McKee," said THE HEAD TEACHER.

"That's all right," said Mrs. McKee. She looked at her daughter. "But what on earth ..."

"Madam," said THE HEAD TEACHER. "We have called you in on a matter of great importance." He held up the page of writing. "May I ask you to read ... this?"

The lovely Mrs. McKee took it from his hand. She read it through. She breathed out the sounds of the nicest words. She sighed. She smiled. She shook her head. She held the page like it was something rather precious.

"This," said THE HEAD TEACHER, "is possibly the most important piece of writing that this young lady will be asked to do all year. It may well be the most important piece of writing that she will do during her time as a student at this school. And she presents us with this!"

Mrs. McKee sighed.

"Oh, Mina," she said. "What are we going to do with you?"

"Don't know, Mum," I said.

And she cuddled me, right there in THE HEAD TEACHER's office while THE HEAD TEACHER and Mrs. Scullery watched. And THE HEAD TEACHER said,

"Mrs. McKee..."

But she raised her hand to stop him.

"You don't need to say anything more, Head Teacher," she said.

"So you understand the gravity of the situation?" said THE HEAD TEACHER.

"Indeed I do," said Mrs. McKee. "So I think I'll take my daughter home now. And I don't think she'll be back for some time. Goodbye."

And we walked out of the office and along the corridor and past the classroom and out of the main door and across the schoolyard and out through the gates into the world.

We walked slowly homeward through the sunlight. We stopped in the park on the way home. We ate ice cream and we sighed at its deliciousness. We sat on a bench by a bush with lovely bright red roses growing on it. We watched people dressed in white playing bowls on the beautiful green lawn. The brown bowls clicked and clunked as they struck each other. The people in white chatted and laughed. Somebody somewhere sang a lovely song. Close by, a little boy rolled down a hill, giggled, got up, ran to his mum and kissed her, then ran up the hill again and rolled down again. It was lovely and warm in the sunshine. The sky was heavenly blue. Bees buzzed. Butterflies flitted by. A dog chased a ball. A flight of honking geese flew over us. The tops of the trees were swaying in the gentle breeze.

"This is very diggibunish," said Mum.

"It is," I said. "And very pringersticks, as well."

When we got home, Mum pinned up GLIBBERTYSNARK in the kitchen. We looked at it together. It was indeed one of the most important pieces of writing I had done all year. I was now a Homeschooled Girl, which made me Very Very Very Very Very Very Pleased. Very.

Mum put her arm around me, and we smiled, and we were filled with claminosity.

EXTRAORDINARY ACTIVITY
Write a page of
UTTER NONSENSE.
This will produce some very fine
NEW WORDS.
It could also lead to some very
SENSIBLE RESULTS.

EGGS, CHICKS, A BELLY, BABIES & POEMS

I am in the tree and the birds have had their eggs! Three of them. They are bluey-green with brownish spots and they are absolutely beautiful! I knew something was up. The birds were silent. The air was still. I climbed higher in the tree, to where I could look down into the nest, and there they were, three of them, lying so prettily in the pretty nest. Bluey-green with brownish spots and they are beautiful. Bluey-green and speckled brown and beautiful. I almost cheered, but I stopped myself. I wanted to hold the birds in my hands and praise them, but of course why should they take notice of me? Why should they care what I might think? But I say it now anyway, deep inside myself: "WELL DONE BLACKBIRDS! YOU ARE EXTRAORDINARY! YOU HAVE CREATED THE MOST AMAZING THINGS IN THE WORLD! YOU HAVE CREATED NEW UNIVERSES!"

Maybe they did hear me somehow, and they certainly saw me, because they squawked their warning calls, so I slithered to my lower branch, where they are used to seeing me and where I can safely be ignored. I sigh with joy.

The chicks are on their way.

And then I see the family outside Mr. Myers's house. The poor boy is as fed up as ever. He's kicking the ground again like he wants to do it harm. Poor lad. Looks like he'd be a perfect candidate for the pills they wanted to give me, or for the Corinthian Avenue Pupil Referral Unit. Cheer up, I want to yell! You've got a mum and dad beside you! You've got a brother or a sister on the way!

The mum and dad are smiling. She holds her belly and I see with that it is egg-shaped. I have to stop myself from jumping out of the tree and running along the street to her and telling her that she is extraordinary.

"YES!" I yell inside myself. "IT'S TIME FOR THINGS TO BE BORN AROUND HERE! BUY THE HOUSE, AND A BABY AND A CLUTCH OF CHICKS WILL BE BORN IN FALCONER ROAD THIS SPRING!"

Maybe she hears me somehow. She turns her head but I'm sure she can't see me because of the foliage around me. O she looks very nice. They all look very nice. They have a key. They open the door, they go inside. I imagine them moving through the dust. I imagine their skin mingling with the skin of Mr. Myers, their breath mingling with his breath, their lives mingling with his life, with his death. I lean back against the tree. I close my eyes. I think about the woman with the egg-shaped belly. And I wonder - if Dad hadn't died, might Mum have had an egg-shaped belly, too?

EGG

I SIT IN

MY TREE, MY KNEES TO

MY CHEST. I EMPTY MY MIND,

AND FORGET THAT MY NAME IS MINA.

I HAVE NO KNOWLEDGE OF THE WORLD. I HAVE NO

KNOWLEDGE OF ANYTHING AT ALL. I AM INSIDE AN EGG.

I AM A SECRET HIDDEN UNMADE THING. A CHICK, GROWING

IN THE STICKY GLOOPY STUFF. TINY BONES AND FEATHERS AND

CLAWS AND EYES AND BRAIN ARE STARTING TO BE FORMED IN

ME. I SIT HERE, FOR A LONG LONG TIME, DEEP IN MY TREE,

DEEP IN MYSELF, DEEP IN MY EGG, CURLED IN THE BLUEY-

GREEN DARKNESS, WAITING FOR THE MOMENT TO

PECK MY WAY OUT, WAITING TO BE BORN

AGAIN, WAITING TO BECOME

A BIRD.

Then I draw: birds and leaves and trees, and I am lost in this, too. Then a goldfinch appears, flickering through the upper branches. Then another, its partner. And I think of last autumn. There were days when a small flock flew through here. They will again when their time comes. I told my mum about them and she then told me that a flock of goldfinches is known as a charm. A charm of goldfinches! How beautiful is that?

I look at today's goldfinch. There it is: black, gold, red, brown, white flickering quickly among the green leaves. There it goes, flying freely away into the blue. Does the goldfinch know how gorgeous it is? Does any bird? Does it know how beautiful its song is? If it did know, then maybe it would try to stop being so gorgeous. It would try not to charm. Once upon a time, goldfinches were the favorites of bird trappers. If the goldfinches knew this, they would have bathed in mud until they were mucky brown. They would have squawked or screeched or they would have stayed silent instead of singing out loud. They would have hidden themselves away in dark and isolated places. They wouldn't have flickered and flashed through people's gardens. They wouldn't have sung their beautiful songs. But goldfinches don't know anything about wickedness or stupidity. And so they flew and sang, and they were trapped in nets, and put into cages, and sold for cash, and they were hung from ceilings or put on sideboards or bookshelves or on windowsills and they sang. And their songs must have been filled with yearning and pain. And their songs lifted over the stupid boring conversations of their stupid boring prison guards. Imagine them! Imagine the stupid boring people who trap birds, who put them into cages! How boring they must be! How stupid they must be! We don't put the goldfinches into cages now. But there are still lots of bird trappers in the world — people who trap the spirit, people who cage the soul. What's a gang of bird trappers called?

A STUPIDITY OF BIRD TRAPPERS!
A BORINGNESS OF BIRD TRAPPERS!
A WICKEDNESS OF BIRD TRAPPERS!
A SCHOOL OF BIRD TRAPPERS!
A SCULLERY OF BIRD TRAPPERS!

They flew away, the charm of goldfinches. Fly, goldfinches! Sing and fly!

Now I sit in the tree and wait. I sit in the blue-green dappled light. I rest my notebook on my knees. I watch Mr. Myers's house. No movement there. I move my pen across the page.

I SIT IN MY TREE
I SING LIKE THE BIRDS
MY BEAK IS MY PEN
MY SONGS ARE MY POEMS.

I play about with my name and my pen and I come up with a concrete poem that shows that Mrs. Scullery was right. Mina McKee truly is hard as iron!

MINA

IRON

NORI

ANIM

I keep on playing with words and my pen. I look at an empty page and it's like an empty sky waiting for a bird to fly across it. I imagine a charm of goldfinches flying freely across it. I imagine them disappearing from sight and the sky, and the page is empty again. Then I think of another bird, a skylark. I imagine it flying upwards on the page. I recall the extraordinary fact that the skylark, unlike any other bird, sings as it rises from the earth, sings as it hovers high in the sky and sings as it drops to ground again. The skylark really does seem to be carried on its song!

SINGS   SINGS SINGS HOVERS SINGS SINGS SINGS
SINGS SINGS   HOVERS SINGS SINGS SINGS HOVERS SINGS HOVERS
HOVERS SINGS AS IT HOVERS HOVERS SINGS HOVERS HOVERS HOVERS
SINGS   SINGS

```
                    IT                          AND
             AS                                 THE
                          SINGS                 SKY
                   AND                          LARK
                          SINGS         SINGS
             AND                                AND
                   SINGS                        SINGS
                   AND                  AND
                   SINGS                        SINGS
                          AND                   AND
             RISES                              SINGS
                          IT                    AND
              AS                                SINGS
                   SINGS                        SINGS
             AND                                SINGS
                          RISES                 SINGS
             IT                                 SINGS
                    AS                  SINGS
                    SINGS                        SINGS
                   AND                          SINGS
                   RISES                        SINGS
                    IT                          AS
              AS                                     IT
                    SINGS                       AS
                    AND                         IT
                    RISES                       AS
              IT                                     IT
             AS                                      FALLS
                    SINGS                    FALLS
                   SINGS                         SINGS
                    LARK                        AS
                          SKY               IT
                    THE                         FALLS
```

T H E   S K Y L A R K

As I write the skylark high above I see Whisper
down below. There he is, prowling in the shadows.
The cat is on the hunt. For mice, perhaps.
For victims.

BLACK BEAST

BLACK BEAST BLACK BEAST
CREATURE OF THE DARK
CREATURE OF THE UNDERWORLD
CREATURE OF THE HOUSES OF THE DEAD
CREATURE VELVET AS THE VELVET NIGHT
BLACK BEAST PROWLING
THROUGH MY WEIRD DREAMS
BLACK BEAST PURRING
IN MY RED RED HEART
BLACK BEAST YOWLING
IN MY YEARNING SOUL
BLACK BEAST BLACK BEAST
YOUR BLOOD IS MY BLOOD
YOUR CLAWS ARE MY CLAWS
YOUR FUR IS MY FUR
YOUR HEART IS MY HEART
YOU CAME TO ME FROM DARKNESS
YOU ARE MY BLACK BLACK BEAST OF DEEPEST DARK
AND YOU ARE WHISPER.

I write for what seems like hours in the blue-green dappled light. And my mind and my hand move smoothly together and I am lost in my thoughts and lost in my words and the minutes pass and the minutes pass, and at the secret hidden center of the blue-green eggs the secret hidden creatures grow.

And then I blink and look up and the family is in the street again. I am hidden from them, and my songs are silent so they don't know that I'm here. I look out through the leaves.

The boy is sullen as always.

The parents are pleased.

They leave in the little blue car.

I watch them leave the street and leave my page.

I think of the mysterious connections between words and the world, and my pen soon moves again, as if I can't stop writing, perched up here beside the blue-green eggs in the blue-green afternoon.

WHO?

I SIT IN MY TREE WITH A BOOK AND A PEN AND I WRITE.
FOR INSTANCE:

"THERE IS A BOY AND A WOMAN AND A MAN IN THE STREET
AND THEY ENTER A HOUSE WHICH ONCE WAS THE HOUSE
OF A MAN CALLED ERNIE MYERS."

FOR INSTANCE:
"THERE IS A CAT NAMED WHISPER WHICH SLINKS PAST THE HOUSE
TO THE OVERGROWN GARDEN AT THE BACK OF THE HOUSE."

FOR INSTANCE:
"THE BLACKBIRDS HAVE MADE THEIR NEST AND THERE ARE
THREE BLUE-GREEN BROWN-SPECKLED EGGS IN IT."

AND SO THEY ALL APPEAR IN MY BOOK:
THE BOY, THE WOMAN, THE MAN, THE CAT,
THE HOUSE, THE GARDEN,
THE BLACKBIRDS, THE TREE, THE EGGS, THE NEST.

AND SOMETIMES I HESITATE.
AND SOMETIMES I WONDER,

IS THERE SOMEONE WHO WRITES,
"THERE IS A GIRL CALLED MINA SITTING IN A TREE."

IS THERE SOMEONE WHO WRITES,
"SOMETIMES SHE HESITATES AND SOMETIMES SHE WONDERS."

AND IF THERE IS, WHO IS IT?
WHO WRITES MINA?
WHO WRITES ME?

SPAGHETTI POMODORO & A DREAM

I could have gone on writing until darkness came, but Mum called me in. I climbed out of the tree. It felt so weird, like I was coming out from a dream. Or like I was coming out from a poem or a story, or like I was a poem or a story myself. Or like I was coming out from an egg! Spaghetti pomodoro helped me to feel ordinary again. Spaghetti pomodoro! I curled it around my fork and plunged it into my mouth. I slurped the dangling threads of pasta. I licked the sauce that dribbled down my chin. I chewed and rolled it all around my mouth. Delicious! So delicious! One of the most delicious things in the known universe!

SPAGHETTI POMODORO!
SPAGHETTI POMODORO!

Mum says that one day we'll go to Italy together and eat spaghetti pomodoro in the land of its birth. We'll have Parmesan cheese and Parma ham and sun-dried tomatoes and polenta and risotto and olives and garlic and fettuccini and ice cream and tiramisu and zabaglione in the land of their birth, where they taste far better than anywhere else. I haven't traveled much yet but Mum says I will, when we can afford it.

When we finish the spaghetti, and the lovely tomatoey garlicky taste is still on our tongues, we sit on the sofa and eat ice cream as the sun goes down outside the window.

I tell her about the blackbirds' eggs and the goldfinches and the family at Mr. Myers's house who look as if they will soon move in.

Then we're quiet, and we watch the sky darkening and reddening as the sun goes down. We see birds flapping nestward. We see an airplane far far away and oh so high. I think of the astounding journeys that birds make across the world. And I think of the journeys I could make one day.

"Bologna," I say softly.

She smiles. Sometimes we do this, just list the names of the places we'll go to one day.

"Andalucia."

"Luxor."

"Trinidad."

"Seaton Sluice."

The reason that we have so little money is that she cut down on the work she did when I left school so that she could care for me properly and have the time to teach me. But she never mentions it. She only says that until the day we set off together, I will have to travel in my mind.

"And in my dreams," I say.

"Yes. You can travel in your dreams."

"To Ashby-de-la-Zouch," I say.

"Or Vladivostok."

"Corryvreckan, Trinidad, Peru."

The sky outside is almost black.

"I found out such an interesting thing today," she says.

"Did you?"

"Yes. It seems that some birds fly right through the night, and sleep as they fly."

"They sleep as they fly?"

"Yes."

"What kind of birds?"

"Swifts, it seems."

I smile at the thought.

"John O' Groats."

"County Kerry."

"Ayers Rock."

"Lhasa."

Later, when I go to bed, I pin some words above my bed and hope to dream.

Sleep
While
I
Fly
Tonight

MINA'S DREAM

At the start, it wasn't really like a dream at all. It was quite like waking up. Mina found herself in her own bedroom, and it was exactly like her own bedroom. Then she realized that there were two Minas. One lay fast asleep in bed, and one was standing at the bedside looking down at the Mina who lay fast asleep in bed.

That's strange, she thought. I'm looking at myself. How can that be?

As she thought this thought, she started to rise towards the ceiling. The Mina in bed did not stir. Mina-who-was-rising saw that there was a kind of shining silver cord that stretched between herself and Mina-on-the-bed. The cord joined the two Minas together, even though they were apart. The Mina who was rising wondered if she should feel scared about what was happening, but really there seemed to be nothing scary about it at all. She looked down at herself, at the pale sleeping face, the closed sleeping eyes, the pitch-black hair. She saw the duvet rising and falling gently as Mina breathed. It all seemed so calm and so comfortable. She smiled, and rose even higher, through the ceiling, into the dark attic space above. She saw the boxes of her old toys that were stacked up there, boxes of her mum's papers, boxes of Christmas decorations and old books. The shining silver cord stretched through the attic floor towards the now-hidden Mina-on-the-bed. And she kept on rising, through the roof itself, and now she was above the house, in the night, with the moon and stars above, and the house and Falconer Road below, and with the silver cord stretching through the roof slates towards Mina-on-the-bed. She gasped, and for a moment the cord seemed to tighten, as if it was about to pull her right back to where she'd come from, but she whispered to herself, "Don't be scared, Mina. Don't stop it now."

And she and the cord relaxed and she rose high above the house, and the street, and she saw the strings of streetlights, and the darkness of the park, and the whole city, and the glimmering river running through it, and the spiral of the motorway, and the roads that ran out toward the moors, and she saw the huge dark sea with the reflections of the moon and stars on it, and a spinning lighthouse light, and the lights of a lonely ship far out upon the seas.

And she laughed.

"I'm traveling!" she said. "I shall go to ... Seaton Sluice!"

And as she said the name of the little seaside town she descended again and found herself hovering above the town she'd been to several times in her waking life. There they all were, the long beach and the turning waves, the white pub on the headland, little tethered fishing boats, the narrow river running into the sea.

The silver cord vibrated and shimmered. It stretched away from her towards where she'd come from, linking Mina-at-Seaton-Sluice to Mina-on-the-bed.

She hovered. She wondered.

"Cairo!" she whispered.

And she rose again, and off she went towards the east, across the North Sea, across the whole of Europe with its great cities and its snow-capped mountains, and she looked down and thought to herself, That must be Amsterdam! The Alps! Milan!

Belgrade! Athens!! And she traveled across the Mediterranean Sea towards the northern shores of Africa, where the sky was beginning to lighten with the dawn.

She saw the great great dusty city of Cairo and heard its din and roar; and saw the pyramids beyond its edge, rising over the desert. She traveled closer. She hovered over the tip of the greatest pyramid. She eased herself gently downward until she stood there, right on the point of the Great Pyramid of Giza, with the other pyramids and the great sphinx and the desert on one horizon and the city of Cairo on the other. And she shivered with the joy of it.

And the silver cord that linked Mina-on-the-pyramid to Mina-on-the-bed suddenly tightened and away she went again, back into the west where it was still true night.

She traveled back over Europe, even more swiftly than she'd come. She paused, high high up, above the clouds that lay like scattered thin veils between herself and the earth. The cities of Europe were like distant star-clusters, like galaxies.

And she streaked down towards Rome. She saw the streetlights, the headlights of a few cars moving through the streets, and with a gasp of delight she saw the floodlit Colosseum and St. Peter's Square and the Trevi Fountain, places she knew only from books until now. Then the cord tugged her harder, faster, and she flew again. The land below was just a blur.

Just one more place! she thought. Durham!

And she saw the cathedral and the castle, the river snaking around them, and to the east the dawn kept rising, rising, as if it was pursuing her. And she sighed and said, "OK! Back home to bed!" And suddenly she was above the park, and the silver cord vibrated and shimmered as it drew her home.

She woke as the early light shone through the window and birds chorused outside.

"Peru," she murmured. "Alice Springs. Vladivostok. I'll go to all those places, too."

EXTRAORDINARY ACTIVITY
Go to sleep.
Sleep while you fly.
Fly while you sleep.

THE STORY OF
CORINTHIAN AVE.

The days are passing quickly. Maybe it will soon be properly spring at last. The family have bought the house. The mum and dad come with stepladders and buckets and mops and brushes. They clean and scrub for hours at a time. Each day I climb high in the tree. Each day the blackbirds squawk, Get back, girl! Squawk! You're danger! Squawk!

Now I'm sitting at the table by my window in my room. And it's time to tell the tale of the Corinthian Avenue Pupil Referral Unit.

When Mum said she wanted to take me out of school and educate me herself, a man and a woman from the council came to the house. I don't remember their names. Ms. Palaver and Mr. Trench, perhaps. They sat together on the sofa and drank tea and nibbled biscuits and tried to look caring and oh-so-concerned. Ms. Palaver (who, I noticed, kept well clear of the fig rolls) watched me out of the corner of her eye. I sat very prim and very proper on a piano stool. They said that legally, Mum was of course well within her rights to make this decision. Did we understand the implications, though? Educating me at home would be quite a drain on

Mum's energy and time. We would not have the facilities of school. I would not have the benefit of company of children of my own age. Mum said we realized those things. We were quite prepared for them. She said we were quite happy about them. And our plan for home education might not last forever.

"Though it might," I said quickly.

Ms. Palaver looked at me in surprise. I looked back at her. She was wearing a black suit with a white blouse and silver earrings. Mr. Trench was also in black and white. I was about to ask them if they were off to a funeral but I thought perhaps not. So instead, somewhat to my own surprise, I said,

"Ms. Palaver."

"Yes, dear?"

"How can a bird that is born for joy sit in a cage and sing?"

Mum gave me a look.

"I'm not certain I understand," said Ms. Palaver.

"Never mind," I said.

I sat up straight again. I looked past Ms. Palaver into the street.

Mum started talking about how Mina had an adventurous mind. She said she'd be able to commit lots of time to Mina. She talked about Mina's dad and about Mina being an only child and about how she had no objections to St. Bede's itself, but ...

"And as for facilities," I said, "we have a very nice tree in the front garden in which I have many thoughts. And the kitchen is a fine laboratory and art room. And who could devise a better classroom than the world itself?"

Mum smiled.

"As you see," she said, "Mina is a girl with her own opinions and attitudes."

Ms. Palaver peered at me closely. I could see her thinking that Mina was an impertinent girl with her own pompous crackpot notions.

"To be quite frank," I said, looking straight back at her, "We feel that schools are cages."

"Indeed?" said Ms. Palaver.

"Yes," I continued. "We feel that schools inhibit the natural intelligence, curiosity and creativity of children."

Mr. Trench rolled his eyes.

Mum smiled and shook her head.

Ms. Palaver said again, "Indeed?"

"Indeed," I said.

"Before you make your final decision, Mrs. McKee," said Mr. Trench, "you might find it worthwhile to have Mina spend a day at Corinthian Avenue."

"Corinthian Avenue?" said Mum.

"It's where we send children who don't ..."

"Or who won't ... ," said Ms. Palaver.

Mr. Trench brought out a leaflet from the inside pocket of his black jacket. He held it out to Mum.

"Can't do any harm," he said.

EXTRAORDINARY ACTIVITY
Read the Poems of William Blake.
(Especially if you are Ms. Palaver.)

The thought of Corinthian Avenue makes me edgy, so I pick up my book and my pen and head downstairs. This is something that needs to be written in the tree! Mum's on the phone in the living room. I get an apple from the fruit bowl and bite into it. I put some trainers on. It looks chilly outside so I put a jacket and scarf on. She's still on the phone.

"I'm going outside!" I call.

She doesn't answer.

"I'm going out, Mum!" I call again.

I listen. I shrug and head for the door. Then she's there, coming out of the living room.

I point to the book and pen.

"Going into the tree," I say.

"OK."

"Who was that?"

"Who was what?"

"On the phone."

"Oh, on the phone? Colin."

"Colin?"

"Colin Pope. Remember? You met him when we went to the theater the other week. In the interval."

"Oh, him."

She folds her arms and tilts her head and looks at me.

"Yes. Him."

I think back. Colin Pope, a skinny tall man with a pint of beer in his hand.

"He was nice, wasn't he? Remember?"

I shrug. I don't remember if he was nice. I hardly remember him at all. Why should I? And anyway, what's nice? He shook my hand and said he'd heard a lot about me. I don't think I said anything to him. I read the program while they prattled and drank and nibbled peanuts. The play was Grimm Tales. I do remember I thought about talking about whether wolves really were as savage as they're made out to be in the fairy tales. But I didn't, and they prattled on.

"Remember him?" Mum says again.

"Not sure if I do," I say.

She grins.

"I'll be off to the tree," I say.

"Go on, then."

I head for the door. I hesitate there.

"What did he want?" I say.

"Just to say hello."

"Took a long time to say hello."

I go out and close the door.

Huh! Colin Pope!

I'm in the tree. The leaves are thickening fast. I check the eggs. Still there, still three of them, still beautiful.

Squawk squawk, go the blackbirds.

"OK," I whisper back.

I sit on my branch, surrounded by thickening leaves. Soon I'll be quite hidden away up here. I turn my mind back towards the past.

They sent a red taxi to take me to Corinthian Avenue – maybe to make sure I went at all. Mum came with me that morning. The taxi driver was wearing a yellow football strip with PELÉ written across the back.

He kept looking at me in the driver's mirror as we set off.

"Do you take many to Corinthian Avenue?" I asked him.

"Sure do. Got a contract. I've took quite a crew to Corinthian Avenue in my time, I can tell you."

He drove on, past the park, through the slow-moving traffic towards the city center.

"And I could tell a tale or two," he said.

"Tell one," I said.

"No chance."

He shook his head. He took a hand off the steering wheel and tapped his nose.

"Confidentiality," he said.

He wound the window down and leaned an elbow on the frame.

"More'n my job's worth," he said.

The traffic thickened, edged through the streets past the offices and shops. We drove slowly onto the bridge. The arch arced beautifully above us. The river sparkled beautifully below.

I caught him watching me again.

"So what's your story?" he said. "If you don't mind me asking, that is?"

"Sorry?"

"Tell me to shut up and stop prying if you like. But some kids like to get it off their chest with a bloke like me. And whatever you say'll stay within these cab walls."

I looked at Mum. She looked at me.

"I think we'll just keep it to ourselves, thank you very much," said Mum.

"It's OK, Mum," I said. "I'm sure Mr. Pelé will keep it secret."

"It's Karl," said Karl.

"OK," I said. "It was violence, Karl."

"Get away," said Karl.

"It's true. I attacked a teacher."

"Aye?"

"Aye. With a pen."

"A pen?"

"Aye. It made a great weapon. I stabbed her in the heart. I'm really vicious once I start. I don't look like it, but I'm a bloody savage!"

I snarled into the mirror. I bared my teeth. Karl raised his eyebrows. He shook his head. He whistled softly.

"Goes to show."

"Goes to show what?"

"That you never can tell."

"That's what I think as well. You never can tell."

He drove on slowly in silence.

"She asked for it," I said.

"Aye?"

"Aye. She went on and on. Yak yak yak."

"Yak yak yak?" said Karl.

"Yes. Yak yak yakkity yakkity yak yak yak."

"I had a teacher like that," said Karl.

"Was she called Mrs. Scullery?"

"Nah. It was a bloke. Blotter, we called him. Can't remember his real name."

"But he went yak yak yak?"

"Aye. He had more of a snarl in it, though. So it was like more vicious. Yek yek yekkity yek! That kind of thing."

"Did you attack him?"

"Naah. He was a great big bloke, and I was just a titch. He had a hell of a temper, and all. So I just shut me lugs and let him get on with it. Yek yek yek yekkity yek."

"Pity. Anyway I'd had enough of Mrs. Scullery and her yak yak yak, so I done her."

"With the pen."

"Aye. I done her good, with the pen."

"Murder?"

"Not quite. She'll survive."

I looked down at the water that flowed beneath us toward the sea. I said,

"Are you as good as Pelé, Karl?"

He grinned.

"Aye," he said. "In fact, I'm even better."

"Really?"

"Really. You should have seen the goal I scored in the park last week. Breathtaking."

We grinned at each other in the mirror.

"So why are you driving taxis?" I said.

"Cos I love it. Who'd want to travel the world and make a million quid and be adored by all them fans? No, it's journeys to Corinthian

Avenue for me! And look, here we are, safe and sound."

He stopped the car and opened the door to let me out.

He pretended to flinch as I stepped out. He put his hands up as if to protect himself.

I laughed and he grinned.

"Keep them pens under control today," he said.

"I will."

"See ya, Miss. Savage."

"Bye-bye, Mr. Pelé."

He winked at us and drove away.

And there it was, a redbrick house surrounded by Tarmac and a steel fence, and tubs with blue hydrangeas in them.

I pause. I need to mess about before I go on. I'll play with words for a while. I'll do a single sentence and a single word. Good games to play while I gather my memories of that day.

A SINGLE SENTENCE

Sometimes when I'm at my table or in my tree and I want to write I start a sentence to see if I can write a whole page before I need a full stop which at first can seem rather difficult but which is really quite easy, because a single sentence could go on forever just like numbers could go on forever, which is difficult for little children to understand because they believe that a number like 100 is so huge that there can be nothing higher until someone says there's 101 and 102 and 103 and they say O yes and so they begin to understand that numbers have no true end and can go on and on and on and on and on and on and on and on and on and on until the end of time, if there is an end of time which I think is maybe impossible because if numbers go on forever maybe time does too, but as I get closer to the foot of the page I know that this sentence must stop very soon which now makes me wonder if I am like God when I am writing and makes me wonder whether God could put an end to time if he decided he has had enough of it and whether one day he will speak the single simple cataclysmic word STOP and everything will simply stop•

A SINGLE WORD

THIS MORNING THE SKY
HAS ONLY
A SINGLE BIRD IN IT.

THIS MORNING MY PAGE
HAS ONLY
A SINGLE WORD ON IT.

SKYLARK

EXTRAORDINARY ACTIVITY
Write a sentence which fills a whole page.

EXTRAORDINARY ACTIVITY
Write a single word at the center of a page.

OK. The Corinthian Avenue Pupil Referral. Unit.
We... No. Not we. Not I. Third person, Mina.
She. They.

MINA AT THE CORINTHIAN AVENUE PUPIL REFERRAL UNIT

And so one day our heroine, Mina, who thought she was so clever and strong, arrived at Corinthian Avenue. As Karl's taxi drove away, Mina walked hand in hand with her mum towards the glass doorway.

As they stepped inside, a woman came to them.

"I'm Mrs. Milligan," she said. "And you must be Mina!"

"Yes, I suppose I must," said Mina.

"She is," said Mina's mum, "and I am Mrs. McKee."

Mrs. Milligan smiled kindly, and led them into a small and brightly lit office. She filled in a form and asked Mina's mum to sign. She opened a file from St. Bede's. Mina sighed and scowled.

"Relax, Mina," said Mrs. Milligan. "We're not here to judge you. We're here to help."

She closed the notes and smiled.

"Didn't really fit in, did you, dear?" she said.

"Hardly."

"One system can't fit us all, can it? We know that here, Mina."

"Do you?"

Mina wanted this woman to be like Palaver or Trench. She wanted her to be like Scullery or like THE HEAD TEACHER. But she was like none of them.

"We know you're only here for a visit," said Mrs. Milligan. "But perhaps you'll like us enough to stay a little longer."

"Or perhaps not," responded the girl.

Mrs. Milligan smiled sweetly. Mina's mum flashed her eyes at Mina. Mina looked away. She was trying to be careless and free, but she was confused, and she was trembling inside. and she felt weirdly quiet, weirdly shy. She wanted to run away.

Mrs. Milligan showed them where the toilets were and where the lunchroom was. Everywhere was neat and clean. There was a cooling smell of lavender. There were lots of books on lots of shelves. There were kids' paintings on the walls. There were stories and poems hanging beside them.

Soon other kids began to arrive in taxis and minibuses. There were adults in T-shirts and jeans with their names on tags that hung around their necks.

Mrs. Milligan took them to Room B12, a room with woodblock flooring, a window with white net curtains on it, tables and red plastic chairs in a ring. One of the walls had a mural painted on it — a huge rain forest with monkeys and snakes and butterflies and frogs. The names of the artists were painted along the bottom edge: Daniela, Eric, Patrick, Steepy ...

"We do a lot of art here," said Mrs. Milligan. "Malcolm's an expert at it. He'll be here soon."

Mina shrugged.

"I hear you're something of an expert, too," said Mrs. Milligan.

"Expert!" grunted Mina.

She rolled her eyes at her mum, who whispered,

"Mina!"

Then Malcolm arrived. He wore blue jeans, a red shirt, a silver bracelet on his wrist.

"I'm Malcolm," he said.

Mina said nothing. Mina's mum nudged her.

"He's Malcolm. You're ..."

"And you must be Mina," continued Malcolm. "I've been looking forward to meeting you."

Mina lowered her eyes. She shuffled her feet. She felt her lips curling downward like on a cartoon face.

"I'm so sorry," said her mum. "She's not usually so ..."

"That's all right!" said Malcolm. "First day, new place, bit shy. She'll be fine once she gets to know us. Ah, Harry! Come and meet Mina."

Harry was a short boy in a blue anorak, with lank hair and perplexed eyes. He came towards them. He nodded shyly at Mina. He held a book out to Malcolm.

"I b-brung it," he said.

"It? Ah, Buddha! Thank you!"

He took the book and fanned it open for Mina.

"One of the first great graphic novels," he said. "As good as they say, Harry?"

"A-aye, Malcolm," stammered Harry. "Aye!"

Mina turned away, as if she disapproved.

"Personally, I prefer the complexity of words," she said. She hated herself even as she was saying it. She had read the book in Malcolm's hands, and she liked it a lot. But she couldn't stop herself from blathering on and showing off and trying to show she was something special, and nothing like the people here.

"The complexity of sentences," she said, "Paragraphs, pages ... "

"Oh, Mina!" said her mum.

Malcolm closed the book.

"Maybe you can make recommendations to us, Mina," he said. "Now, Mrs. McKee, why don't you leave Mina with us, and ... "

"Yes, I will," said Mrs. McKee.

She gave Mina a hug. She told her to have a nice day. She told her she'd be back to pick her up that afternoon.

As she walked away, Mina wanted to weep like a four-year-old. She wanted to cry, "Take me away, Mummy! Take me away!" But she just stood there, like a stone, silent and bereft.

And other children started to arrive, and so the day began.

Among the others, there was Wilfred, who looked so angry, whose brow was furrowed, who clenched his fists, who looked nobody but Malcolm in the eye. His nails had almost been bitten to nothing and two of his front teeth were gone. He smelt of dog.

There was Alicia, who took a liking to Mina and sat by her all day. Alicia was like a little creature. Her hands trembled, ever so slightly. Her fringe hung down over her eyes. She kept leaning forward so that her hair hung all around her head like a curtain. She spoke in little whispery breaths. "I like you, Mina. Can I sit with you at lunch, Mina?" She stayed silent mostly, but sometimes Mina would hear her humming a low slow tune.

And there was Steepy, a skinny boy dressed all in green whose hands were covered in cuts and grazes. "Bloody roses, Malcolm," he said. "Covered in bloody thorns, Malcolm. And bloody brambles. Like bloody knives, Malcolm." He grinned at Mina. "It's me bloody garden, Nina."

"Mina," said Malcolm. He winked. "It's Steepy's aim to have the most abundant allotment in the land. It's also his aim to get a swearword into every sentence."

"Bloody right, Malcolm," said Steepy. "Couldn't write a sentence to save me bloody life, but when it comes to swearing versatility ... And when it comes to works of bloody art ... "

He lifted his shirt. There was a whole garden tattooed on his chest: hedge, trees, dozens of flowers, butterflies, birds.

"That's just the bloody start. I'll get a bloody forest on me legs, mountains on me back, bloody sky on me bloody head."

Despite herself, and her determinationto stay cool and distant, Mina leaned forward wide-eyed.

"But you're just a boy!" she heard herself saying.

"Aye, and I had it done when I wasn't even twelve. Me uncle Eric done it. He's a proper tattoo artist. They wanted to lock him up but they didn't cos he's all I've got. But he can't do no more tattoos on me till I'm sixteen. Then I'll get the rest." He lowered his shirt again. "We're messing up the bloody world, Mina. We're gonna burn it, blow it up, destroy it. We're killing everything. Every lovely living thing'll be extinct. But it'll all be on me, Mina. I'll be a bloody monument to everything that's gone."

"He's not as pessimistic as he makes out," said Malcolm. "Otherwise why bother with all the gardening?"

"For love," said Steepy.

"Bloody love, you mean," said Malcolm.

"Aye. For bloody love." He looked at Mina. "What's your story, then?"

Mina shrugged.

"What's yours?" she said.

"You've had it. What's the point of school when there's bloody gardening to be done?"

"What you doing here, then?"

"Hanging out with me mates. Like Malcolm. And Wilfie there."

Wilfred glared. He bared his teeth. Steepy raised his hand.

"Down, boy," he said. "You are me bloody mate, Wilf, whether you want to be or not."

Wilf went on glaring, looking nothing like a mate of anyone's at all.

Steepy winked at her.

"He's OK," he whispered. "As long as he keeps taking the pills."

"The pills?"

"Aye. They wanted to put me on them as well. No bloody way! I said. Bloody pills!"

Despite herself, she wanted to be his mate, too. She did want to tell him her story, and to hear more about his, to talk about his garden and his tattoo, and to ask him how a bird that was born for joy could sit in a cage and sing, and to tell him about charms of goldfinches. She wanted to tell him about playing with words on a page, and about the words she used to write on her own skin. And she wanted to tell him that they'd wanted to put her on pills, as well. But she didn't. She went back to being distant. She turned away from him to Alicia, who smiled and touched her arm and softly hummed.

"So," said Malcolm. "That's getting to know

you time over. Time for Maths. Sorry, Steepy. Bloody Maths."

They did worksheets at the tables. A couple of assistants came in, Chloe and Joe. Chloe sat with Mina and guided her through the problems. "7 x 6 is the same as 6 x __." "123 x 9 is the same as 9 x __." They were easy. She heard Wilfred curse out loud and fling his pen across the room. He stood up and stormed to the window waving his fists. She saw Malcolm gently guide him back to his task again. She heard Steepy speaking the answers to Malcolm and saw Malcolm writing them down. Alicia sat beside Mina and whispered how she always found sums so hard. Mina helped her and she saw the tears turn to smiles as the solutions appeared to her. She also saw the thin scars on Alicia's forearms. She touched one of them gently. Alicia flinched, then whispered very softly, "I used to cut meself, Mina. Not no more, though." Mina looked through Alicia's hanging fringe into her eyes. She wanted to tell her about the day when she was in her tree, carving words into the bark with her knife. She had rested the blade on her own skin. She was almost at the point of carving a word into herself. She didn't tell her, though.

Alicia smiled sadly.

"I seen sense," she said.

"Me, too," whispered Mina. "Let's do more sums."

Mina went on helping Alicia with her work. She kept glancing around the room, watching these people she had found herself with. A bunch of misfits in a place that accepted them as misfits. She knew them, she understood them. It was so weird. The kids she was with all had trouble fitting in anywhere, but here in a place of misfits they were accepted and they all kind of fitted in and for a few hours in the day they weren't misfits anymore. And there were other rooms with other misfits all around them. Troubled, damaged, shy, scared children. Kids with pains and problems and yearnings. She tried to stop herself thinking it, but she couldn't stop herself. She recognized these kids. In some way, they were just like her. But she kept on trying to stay distant.

At lunchtime, she ate macaroni cheese and chocolate cake. She walked around the concrete playground in the sunlight with Alicia. She stood at the fence and stared towards the city that she'd come from. She wondered about her mum, where she was, what she was doing. She found herself thinking about what Steepy had said, that one day everything she saw would be destroyed. But could that be true? There couldn't be total destruction, there couldn't just be nothing. Yes, maybe one day the human race would be extinct just like the dinosaurs. And our cities would crumble into dust. We'd destroy the Heaven we'd helped to make. But there'd be survivors.

The birds flew over her, sparrows and finches and crows: light-boned, beautiful creatures. They were fragile-looking things, but maybe they were really the strongest and the bravest of all. Surely they'd outlast us, like they outlasted the dinosaurs. They'd keep on flying, building their nests, singing their songs, laying their eggs, tending their young in the ruins of our cities and in our rampant woods and fields. A new wild world would grow around them. And maybe they'd be the ancestors of marvelous creatures that we could have no notion of. She imagined a future world, a future heaven, inhabited by marvelous birdlike creatures, and she was glad.

Malcolm came to her and asked if she was enjoying herself. Yes, she told him. He said they'd be writing stories that afternoon — her kind of thing, he thought. She just shrugged again and said nothing. He told her he had a secret that hardly anybody knew. He'd written a novel and he was trying to get it published. He said how scary it was, like he was exposing himself to the world and it made him feel really stupid and young.

"Know what I mean?" he said.

She shrugged.

"Yes," she said.

"But I've just got to be brave about it," he said. "Haven't I?"

"Suppose so."

He smiled gently at her. She looked away.

"I think you're brave," he said. "I think all of you are brave, coming to places like this, trying to grow up. It's hard, isn't it?"

"What is?"

"Trying to discover how to be yourself."

She nodded.

"There's many ways to do it, Mina. A different way for each and every one of us. And you know what? It goes on all your life."

She said nothing. She watched a flock of pigeons flying fast across the rooftops.

"We don't mind if you think we're not the place for you," said Malcolm. "Whatever you decide, it's nice to have you with us, even if it's just for a short time. It's nice to have been part of your growing."

She looked down at her feet.

"What's it called? The novel?"

"Joe Carter's Bones. It's about a boy who collects all kinds of bones that are lying in the streets and fields around him — birds, mice, frogs. And he gets feathers and bits of leather and grass and leaves and petals and sticks, all kinds of stuff that were part of living things. Puts them together in his shed. Shapes them into things that look like they could live. Tries to breathe life into them again. Tries to make new kinds of creatures with them."

"Like a magician."

"Aye. Like a magician, a sorcerer." Malcolm laughed. "Sounds barmy, eh?"

"Does it work?"

"Does he make a new creature, you mean? Yes, he does, which makes it even barmier. The book's a bit like that, I suppose. It's all bits and pieces, fragments put together to try to make a work of art. I put the bits of the book together and breathe on them and try to make them live. Just like Joe Carter does with his bones." He laughed again. "And the book keeps getting rejected, so maybe it's too barmy for anybody to publish. Maybe next time I should write a story where everything's plain and simple and straightforward. Maybe I should write a book where nothing barmy happens at all, eh? Or where nothing of any kind happens at all?"

She smiled at the idea.

"Do you think you could?" she said. "Write a story where nothing happens at all?"

"Dunno, really. But maybe I should try it. Or maybe you should."

And then a bell rang, and they walked back

across the concrete towards the classroom.

They did do stories that afternoon. Malcolm kept lifting objects, showing them, making the kids imagine stories from them. He lifted a pen and said it belonged to a girl called Maisie and when she wrote with it, it had magic powers. He asked, What were the magic powers? And the possible magic powers appeared in the kids' minds. Then he asked about Maisie's life — the injured pet she had when she was six, her favorite food, why had she fallen out with her best friend, Claire, last week, the scary dream she had last week — and Maisie's whole life began to appear in their imaginations. He lifted other objects — a key that had saved Billy Winston's life. How had it done that? And what secret letter did Billy keep in his drawer? And how did Billy Winston break his wrist when he was seven? He showed an ordinary hen's egg. What if, when it opened, it wasn't a chicken that appeared at all, but some unknown beast? And on and on. He showed how our brains make stories naturally, that they find it easy. He said that stories weren't really about words — the words that kids like Wilfred and

Steepy found so difficult to control. They were about visions. They were like dreams. Mina loved all this. She scribbled the answers, the fragments of stories. She loved to see all the new characters and their worlds coming to life inside her mind and on her page.

When Malcolm asked them to begin to write, as Steepy and Wilfred and Alicia murmured their visions to Malcolm and the assistants and watched visions transformed into words, Mina kept wondering: What if there was a story where nothing interesting happened at all?

So she tried to do that. But of course each time she wrote a word, something started to happen. As soon as she named a character, the character started to come to life and walked around in her head and on the paper. There was no way to write anything and make it into nothing. Maybe writing was a bit like being God. Every word was the start of a new creation. She wrote sentence after sentence, threw away sentence after sentence. Close by her, Steepy told a tale about a dragon called Norman hatching from an egg. Wilfred muttered about the gang of thugs that chased Billy Winston into a dilapidated warehouse, Alicia sighed about Maisie's cat that had almost been run over when it was just a kitten.

Mina kept her eyes lowered, and she listened. Everyone around her seemed to fit in here. For a moment she hated herself. She was useless. She was silly, and endlessly contrary. She fitted in nowhere, even in a place designed for misfits. She looked back at the page and realized that the only story in which nothing happened was a story that wasn't written at all. It was an empty page. Knowing that made her lonely and scared. Sometimes she wished just for this — to be nothing, to be nowhere, to be empty. Sometimes she wanted a life in which nothing at all had happened to her. Sometimes she wished she was like a story that had never even started. Malcolm was right. As well as being wonderful and exciting, growing up could just be hard, so bloody hard.

The voices murmured and sometimes laughed around her. She tried to shut them out. She looked

into the page and visions and memories moved
across it. She saw herself at home again, sitting in
her tree again. She saw her mum in a cafe, drinking
coffee. She thought of her dad deep down below
inside the darkness of the earth and of him gazing
down from high above in Heaven. And there was the
murmuring of Alicia and Wilfred's rage and Harry's
shyness and the images on Steepy's chest, and
Malcolm's kindness and his vivid shirt and his silver
bracelet glinting at the edge of her vision. And the
memory of Palaver and Trench started flooding in,
and Scullery and THE HEAD TEACHER, and SATS
Day, and God and flesh and emptiness, and stories
in which life itself is created from old bones and
stories in which nothing at all happens and and and
and and and and and ... And maybe it was all these
things together, all those bits and pieces from the
present and the past, that disturbed everything and
caused the visionto appear. Whatever it was, she
looked up, and looked through the window into the
sunlight pouring down onto the concrete courtyard
outside, and she saw him.

He was standing at ease on the concrete

close by a couple of parked cars. He was tall and smiling and just like she seemed to remember he was like in life. The air seemed to crackle like fire around him. He turned his head, and looked into Room B12 at the Corinthian Avenue Pupil Referral Unit, and he looked at Mina, who watched him from inside. And he smiled at her, not a sweet and gentle smile but a smile that seemed to go right to a place where all her dreams were. He was in her mind and heart, her body and blood, and she knew that despite everything, everything was OK. Then he was gone, fading into the crackle of fire around him, and there was just concrete and cars and the air and the sun and the emptiness of the Corinthian Avenue afternoon.

She stared into the emptiness for a while. Then she blinked and looked around her. No one had seen anything. They worked on, bathed in the sunlight that poured in through the windows.

She put her pen on the empty page and wrote,

"At Corinthian Avenue I saw my dad and I was glad."

Corinthian Avenue wasn't for me. I enjoyed the day, I learned a lot. It taught me that misfits can fit together in weird ways. It taught me that one day even as a misfit I might fit into this weird world. I liked the people there. I would always remember Steepy and the garden on his chest. But it wasn't the right time. I needed to be at home with my mum, with my tree. I needed to be homeschooled. After the story-writing, Malcolm read the pieces out to everyone, and we heard about dragons and murders and scared kittens and wonderful imaginary lives. We all laughed and groaned and said how brilliant the stories were. When it was my turn, I put the words about my dad away and held up an empty page. I looked at everyone properly for the first time that day.

"My story," I said, "is an empty page. It is a story in which nothing happens at all."

They all looked at the page. They all looked at me. They thought about what I'd said, and I smiled when I thought what Mrs. Scullery might say to such a thing.

"It's like my back," said Steepy suddenly.

"Like your back?" I said.

"Aye. It's empty now. But you know that it'll be filled with something bloody marvelous one day."

"Filled with possibilities, in other words," said Malcolm.

"Yes," said Steepy. "So it isn't really empty at all." He laughed at me. "So even a blank page has a kind of story in it."

We all agreed that that was so.

Soon the day ended.

As I was getting ready to leave, Steepy came to me.

"You won't come back, will you?"

I shrugged, and looked down.

"You won't. But mebbe you will one day. We could be good mates, you and me."

"Could we?"

"Aye. We could."

Alicia came to me as well. She touched my cheek. She said goodbye. I touched her arm.

"I almost did what you did," I said, so softly she could hardly hear. She knew what I was

242

talking about, though.

"But you seen the sense," she said. "Just like me."

We smiled at each other.

"Yes," I said. "Like you."

Mum came back. We thanked Malcolm and Mrs. Milligan for our day. Karl came and drove us homewards.

"So," he said. "Was there much yak yak yakkity yak?"

"No."

"Good."

"And did you attack anybody?"

"Nobody at all."

"Well done."

"Thank you, Mr. Pelé."

Mum put her arm around me. I was occupied with myself, filled with memories of the day and thoughts of what I'd do tomorrow.

"Well?" she said. "Did you settle down? You were being very strange when I left this morning."

"Just uncomfortable, I suppose."

"But you settled down."

I sighed.

"Yes," I told her. "The people were very nice. I had a good time. I ..."

I hesitated, looked out at the traffic. For some reason, there was no way I could tell her about my vision.

She smiled.

"But it's not for you?"

I shrugged.

"No. I'm sorry, Mum."

"I don't mind."

"Really?"

"Really, Mina. I didn't really think it would be, somehow. Come on, cuddle in."

I cuddled into her. I told her about Steepy and Malcolm and the others. I saw Karl smiling at us through the driver's mirror. I closed my eyes, and saw Dad again inside me, standing in the crackling sunlight. One day I'd tell her, but not yet. When I look back now, I suspect that Mum had her own secret that afternoon. I recall how happy she felt against me. I remember seeing her smile to herself as we drove back across the river. Was it Colin Pope? Had she taken the chance to be with him that day, freed from her weird daughter? I suspect she had.

And so I leave the tree, and go back into the house. Mum's sitting at the table reading a book about the Antarctic.

"Hi," she says.

"Hi." I take a breath. "I do remember Colin Pope," I say.

"Do you?"

"Yes. And I remember he seemed very nice, Mum."

She smiles.

"Good. He is."

"And," I said softly, "I think you're very brave."

She laughed.

"I'm not," she said. "But thank you, love."

A STORY
WITHOUT
WORDS

On the next page is the story I created at Corinthian Avenue. It's an empty page, no words at all. It's like Steepy's back, waiting for tattoos. It's like an empty sky waiting for a bird to cross it. It's as silent as an egg waiting for the chick to hatch. It's like the universe before time began. It is like the future waiting to become the present. Look at it closely, and it can be filled with memories, with dramas, with dreams, with visions. It's filled with possibilities, so it isn't really blank at all.

CHICKS, A LETHAL CAT & LIMPLESSNESS

The black beast is on the prowl. Be very wary. Because the black beast really is a black black beast. It's a pretty purring pet called Whisper but it's also a wild thing that will kill if we give it the chance. That's because the eggs have hatched! There are three pretty sticky feathery things inside the pretty nest! And the parent birds are flying back and forwards with fleas and flies inside their mouths, with worms dangling like fat spaghetti from their beaks. I've climbed carefully, quietly, just high enough to look down and see the extraordinary pretty things. And the parents squawked at me – Squawk squawk squawk! – and tilted their heads as they looked at me.

Don't you dare! they squawked. Keep away! Squawk! You're danger! Squawk!

But the real danger's down below. The black beast's prowling in the garden. It's slinking along the pavement. It tries to look casual and unconcerned, but it hesitates and listens. I see it turning its head, turning its ear towards the nest. And it looks up at me with O so pleading eyes.

Hello, Mina, purrs the black black beast. I'm

your special friend, aren't I? I'm your lovely little pet. Why don't you let me come up there to keep you company?

I glare back down, and I point my finger.

Don't you dare, you black black beast! Keep away! You're danger!

I wave it off and it turns in a huff and prowls haughtily away. It'll soon be back, making eyes at me, and licking its teeth at the thought of crushing the pretty little things inside its mouth.

I sit still in the tree. I tell myself I'm the Guardian of the Chicks. But I'm not really. In truth, the chicks are safe inside the nest. They're out of Whisper's reach. He couldn't climb up here. And even if he could, he couldn't climb out to where the nest is. It's built on branches far too thin to hold him. So he prowls below, listening, watching, waiting. The real time of danger will come when the chicks are fledged, when they're out of the nest but not able to fly well, when they're hiding in the hedges and the shadows and the parent birds are still feeding them.

It's safe to close my eyes. I stop being the

Guardian of the Chicks and I try again to imagine being inside an egg. I imagine the sticky feathers and wings growing on me. I imagine peck peck pecking at the shell with my little pointy beak. I imagine pecking my way out the blue-green darkness of the egg into the blue-green light of the tree, just like the chicks have done. I imagine testing my tiny chirping voice for the first time. And I make tiny, almost-silent tweets and squeaks, pretending that my throat is a bird's throat and my mouth is a beak and ...

And then I hear my name spoken.

"Mina? Mina?"

I open my eyes. I look down. There's a girl standing just underneath me. She's wearing a St. Bede's sweatshirt.

"Mina."

I can't speak. I make a rather silly-sounding tweeting noise. I bite my lip.

"Do you not remember me, Mina?"

I nod. Of course I do. It's Sophie Smith, the girl from school, the girl that was my friend for a while.

"Yes," I squeak at last.

"Just thought I'd come and say hello," she says. She smiles. "Hello."

"Hello," I squawk.

She smiles again, looks up at me in my tree. Blue eyes, blond hair, pale face. Just like she was, but older. The blackbirds are squawking in alarm at this new visitor.

"They've got chicks," I cheep.

Sophie smiles.

"Just being good parents," she says. She widens her eyes. "I won't harm them!" she whispers up towards the birds.

Squawk! go the birds. Squawk! Squawk!

"Brave things," says Sophie. "And soon they'll be brave enough to let their babies fly away."

Then she flaps her arms and jumps and jumps.

"Look!" she says. "I had my operation!"

"That's good."

She strides in a confident small circle on the pavement.

"It's not totally fixed yet," she says. "But it is nearly."

"That's fantastic. Did it hurt?"

"Yes. And still does, a bit." She strides a circle again. She kicks her feet and sways her hips. "But it was worth it."

"That's great, Sophie."

My voice sounds so small, really like a little chick's.

"Did you have yours?" she says.

"Pardon?"

"Your operation. The destrangification operation. Remember?"

"O. Yes, I remember. No, I haven't had it yet."

"Still strange, then?"

"I suppose so."

She smiles.

"That's good. You might still come back, though?"

"Pardon?"

"You might come back to school? I often wonder about you."

I look at the leaves around me. I suddenly feel so stupid up here. I feel so small and so

inarticulate. She wonders about me? I haven't a
clue what to say.

"I don't know," I mutter. "No, I don't
think so. I think that schools are ..."

My voice trails away. I can't even finish the
sentence.

"Even Mrs. Scullery said it might be nice if
you came back again," says Sophie.

"Scullery? You're joking!"

"No."

"Huh!"

Someone calls Sophie's name. I look along
the street. Three girls are there, at the far end,
sitting on a low garden wall.

"Sophie! Come on!"

"I have to go," she says. She laughs. "You're
crackers, aren't you?"

Again I hardly know what to say.

"Am I?" I squeak.

"Yes. But you're nice. And I'm crackers as
well in my way. So are lots of us."

"Are you?"

"Yes."

I bite my lip again. I stare down at her, then I glance at the girls along the street. Can it be true?

"Well," says Sophie. "Maybe we're not quite as crackers as you are. But crackers anyway."

"Sophie!" they call again.

She shrugs and smiles.

"Nothing wrong with being crackers, is there?"

"No," I squeak.

"If you did come back, I'd help you."

"Thank you," I whisper.

"Anyway," she says. She does a couple of jumps on the pavement. "I just wanted to show you my limplessness!"

She jumps and jumps again.

"Limplessness," I whisper. "Limp-less-ness!"

"Not bad, eh?" says Sophie.

"No. Not bad. Very good."

"And I just wanted to say hello. And now goodbye."

Then she's gone. I say goodbye after her. I want to jump down and run after her and grab her and tell her she's nice, too, and that I'm very pleased for her, and that ... But I don't. She goes back to her friends. I close my eyes.

"Stupid Mina!" I squeak to myself.

"She wonders about me," I squawk softly.

"She says I'm nice," I whisper.

"Limplessness," I murmur, and I slowly write two lovely words in my book.

LIMPLESSNESS!
DESTRANGIFICATION!

There they are, two brand-new words brought into the world by Sophie Smith and written in my book by me. So maybe she is crackers, too, as she says she is.

She's gone from the street with her friends.

I write again, so shyly, so timidly.

Sophie's nice. I wish she had stayed a little longer. I wish I had asked her to stay a little longer. Silly silly Mina!

I think about what Sophie said about Mrs. Scullery and this gets me to thinking about Mrs.

Scullery and I write again.

A CONFESSION. OK, maybe Scullery wasn't quite so horrible and screechy as I made her out to be. And maybe THE HEAD TEACHER wasn't quite so thick. And maybe they both showed a bit more understanding than I said they did. But when you're writing stories, sometimes you just have to do these things. You have to EXAGGERATE, otherwise there wouldn't be any DRAMA. It's just what writers DO!! OK?

Weird, how I can feel so frail and tiny sometimes, and other times so brave and bold and reckless and free, and ... Does everybody feel the same? When people get grown-up, do they always feel grown-up and sensible and sorted out and ... And do I want to feel grown-up? Do I want to stop feeling ... paradoxical, nonsensical? Do I want to stop being crackers? Do I want to be destrangified? O yes, sometimes I want nothing more – but it only lasts a moment, then oh I want to be the strangest and crackerest of everybody, to be... O stop it, Mina! Sometimes I just think too much and ponder too much and ... Stop it, I said!

Then there's no time to squeak or squawk or wish or wonder anything else because a great big white van pulls into the street and stops outside Mr. Myers's house. Then the blue car pulls up behind it and the family gets out. The mum has the baby all wrapped up in white in her arms.

"Already?" I whisper.

She looks along the street. She holds the baby close like she wants to protect it from the world. The dad moves close and hugs them both. I hear the baby crying. She carries it inside. I imagine them in there, in the still-half-dilapidated house, the brand-new baby, the ancient neglected place.

Then the doors of the van open and the dad and two burly men start carrying furniture into the house.

The boy stays all alone, glaring at the earth, glaring at the sky. He holds a football under his arm.

"What do you wish?" I whisper to him, and of course there's no way for him to hear.

The new boy looks nice, I tell myself. Will I be brave enough to tell him that? Does he go to school? Of course he does.

He bounces the ball, once, twice. He kicks it against the garden wall, once, twice. He glares at the street as if he hates it. Then he does follow his family and the furniture inside.

I keep on watching. Then Mum's below me, smiling up at me.

"I see the newcomers have arrived," she says.

We look along towards Mr. Myers's house, which is no longer Mr. Myers's house.

"And the baby," I say.

"The baby? Already?"

"Yes."

"Oh dear. I suppose they hoped to be more prepared. But they come when they come."

"And the eggs have hatched as well," I say.

"So it's the right time. It's a day of chicks and babies!"

She reaches a hand towards me.

"And listen to me, my baby."

"Yes?"

"I think maybe you're too much up there

in your tree."

"Too much in the tree?"

"Yes. You should come down into the world
a bit more. And you should come down and come
for a walk with me."

"A walk to where?"

"To wherever our feet might take us."

"OK."

I drop down, out of the tree. Then I put
my finger to my lips.

"Listen," I whisper.

"To what?"

"Just listen. If we listen closely we'll maybe
hear the chicks cheeping in the nest. Maybe we'll
even hear the baby."

We listen closely, closely, closely. We stretch
upwards, turn our heads towards the nest.

"Hear them?" I say.

She shakes her head.

"Me neither," I say.

We grin at each other.

"Maybe tomorrow," I say. "Take us
somewhere, feet."

WALKING, PIZZA, STARS & DUST

We walk out of the street into the park. She says this is an educational walk with educational content. Palaver and Trench have asked for a report on what we've been up to. So she will tell them about my writing, my research into birds, our artwork etcetera etcetera etcetera etcetera. She will tell them how even walks in the park can be deeply educational.

"So let's walk," she says, "and think about a theory about walks by Paul Klee."

"Who's he?"

"One of the great artists of the twentieth century. He said that drawing was taking a line for a walk."

I thought about that, about the way a pencil point moves across paper as you draw.

"So if drawing is like walking," I say, "then walking is like drawing."

"Yes, and if you think of it like that, it allows you to wander and to roam and to explore."

I smile at the loveliness of that. I imagine our feet leaving a drawing behind us. I swerve and skip to add curves and interest to our drawing.

"People said that Klee's paintings looked like they could have been done by a child," she says. "Some people hated them. The Nazis, for instance. Burn the lot! they said."

I listen, and I think some more.

"Maybe writing's like walking as well," I say. "You set off writing like you set off walking and you don't really need to know where you're going till you get there, and you don't know what you'll pass along the way."

She smiles.

"So writing's like taking some words for a walk," she says.

"It is."

We walk on, close together, our feet moving in rhythm with each other's. I imagine each step as a syllable, and I breathe the words as I step along.

Each word is a step a-long the way to I don't know where

"Picasso loved Klee's work," Mum says. "He said it took years to learn how to paint like a master, and a lifetime to learn to paint like a child."

It's so strange: grown-ups trying to become young, young ones trying to grow up and all the time, whatever people want, time moves forwards, forwards.

I walk the words.

A life-time to learn to paint like a child

A life-time to learn to paint like a child

"Wordsworth used to write as he walked," she says.

"Did he?"

"Yes. He said that the rhythm of walking helped him to find the rhythms of his poetry."

"Makes sense."

"It does."

To write is to take some words for a walk

The words foll-ow the rhy-thm of the feet

The feet foll-ow the rhy-thm of the words

To write is to take some words for a walk

"And walking's also a kind of meditation," she says.

"Is it?"

"Yes. Meditation's often about sitting very still and keeping the mind very still."

"Like I do in the tree sometimes?"

"Yes. But there is also walking meditation. You concentrate on every step. You think of nothing else. You do nothing but walk. You hope to become clear and calm."

We try it. We walk side by side along the pathway through the park. Now I don't think about words or lines. I try to think of nothing but taking one step then another step then another step. We breathe slowly and regularly.

"Now think about nothing," she says. "Just walk while you walk."

But as we walk through the park, I suddenly can't help thinking of the tunnel underneath and I get agitated instead of calm. Mum knows somehow. She stops. She looks at me. She waits. I find myself telling her about the day that I ran out of school and went down there all alone and saw the man and the dog. I tell her I thought I'd be able to go down there and bring Dad back, that I was trying to do what Orpheus was trying to do. I manage to laugh about it as I tell her.

"I must have been so stupid," I tell her. "I

must have been so young."

I keep on trying to laugh, but I'm nearly crying now.

She holds me tight.

"You should have told me at the time," she says.

"I'm telling you now."

"And you really saw a dog?" she asks me.

"Yes. A man and a dog. I thought the dog was Cerberus. I thought the man was some kind of guardian of the Underworld. I thought I was going down to Hades!"

"Oh, Mina!"

I manage to laugh again.

"He was probably just one of the workmen," I say. "The dog was probably just a stray."

I even manage to giggle now.

"Take me further, feet," I say, and we keep on walking in the light as I remember walking in the dark.

"I thought if I kept on walking and walking," I tell her, "I'd see Pluto and Persephone!"

"Oh, Mina! What a girl!"

"I had it all planned in my mind, I think," I say.

"And what would you have said to Pluto and Persephone?"

I laugh.

"Give him back! Give him back!"

She shakes her head.

"Give him back!" she murmurs.

We keep on walking. We're silent for a while. We listen to the birds and the city all around us.

She asks if I'm OK, if I'm really OK.

"Yes."

I want to shut up but I find myself telling her about Sophie's visit as we walk.

"That was nice of her," says Mum. "Maybe she'll come again."

"Maybe."

"Maybe she could be your friend again."

I shrug.

"Maybe."

And I want to be clear and calm but I find myself thinking about the boy from the family standing in the street, and I find myself telling her about him, too.

"And does he look interesting?" she says.

I shrug.

"Maybe."

She smiles and seems about to say something more, but then she just takes my hand and squeezes it and says, "I'm sure he is."

I turn my mind away from the underworld and from Sophie and the boy. I concentrate on the calming rhythm of walking.

My feet will take me where they wish to go
My feet will take me where they wish to go
My feet will take me where they wish to go

As I breathe the syllables at every step, the rhythm turns the words into a kind of music. The walking turns into a kind of walking dance.

We don't ask each other where we should walk, but we walk upwards, on the pathway by the stream that runs through the park. It rushes and gurgles at our side. A road bridge carries noisy traffic over us. We pass a little field where boys are playing football and yelling wildly at each other. "Cross it! To him! To me! On me head! Yesss! Oh, no!" We come to the little petting zoo where there are little goats with little horns and potbellied pigs and beautiful glistening noisy peacocks. There are tiny children sitting in buggies, and toddlers holding their mums' hands. They lean down and whisper to the goats and pigs, just like I once did, and I watch, and it's like looking back through time. I think of the new baby in the street. I think of the baby as "she." She will come here, before too long, to lean down and whisper at the goats and pigs. Maybe I will bring her here. Maybe I will hold her hand and walk with her through the park and take her home again. I catch my breath at the joy of the thought of that. A little girl in our street. A little girl to be my friend!

We walk again. We climb the path towards the exit from the park. The birds are noisy in the hedges and the undergrowth. We step through the park gate. There's a parade of small shops outside. A hairdresser named Kurl Up 'n' Dye, a Chinese takeaway named Wok This Way, and Pani's Pizza & Pasta Place.

We keep on walking. We don't ask where we

should walk to but we both know where we're going now. We pass the shops. We walk by a busy road.

The traff-ic is so noi-sy at our side
The traff-ic is so noi-sy at our side
The traff-ic is so noi-sy at our side

We arrive at another set of massive gates and we step through into the graveyard. We pause for a moment. So many graves, so many bodies, so many souls, so many people gone. Rows and rows and rows of them. And monuments, and angels, and crosses, and flat tables, and carved names and dates, and pots with flowers in them, and a great big sky above. And people like us, walking slowly by the graves, standing still, leaning down at particular ones, whispering and praying.

We hold each other's hand and walk again. We come to Dad and stand there side by side.

"Hello, Dad," I whisper.

"Hello, love," Mum whispers, too.

I pick up a sweet wrapper that's blown onto the ground above him. Mum tugs away a little weed. I remember him holding me as he read to me. Mum closes her eyes, clasps her hands, remembering, too, I suppose, or praying, or maybe even telling him about Colin Pope.

I love you, Dad, I whisper.

I do shed a tear. I do know that wherever he is or whatever he is now, there's no way for him to come back again. There's no Underworld to go to. There's no Pluto to go to. But it's lovely standing there, the two of us, sharing the memory of Dad. I think of his breath in the air around us, the molecules of his water in the drifting clouds, the echo of his words in my memory as he read to me.

The sky's so huge, so blue. There are blackbirds singing, and a single loud and lovely lark. I try to see it, but it's so so high and so far away that it can't possibly be seen. I look down again and a single white feather is tumbling slowly past our feet. Mum stoops down and catches it. She presses it against my shoulder.

"A perfect fit," she says. "Must be one of yours, Mina."

"Must be."

She hands it to me. I spread my arms and pretend to fly, holding the feather out with my fingertips. Then I let the feather go. It falls slowly towards the earth and drifts away again across the pathways and graves.

"Now the breeze is taking the feather for a walk," I say. "And it won't know where it's going till it gets there."

We stay a little longer. We murmur more words, then we whisper goodbye and we walk away.

Time's passing fast. The sky's already reddening as it heads to dusk. I feel so light, so loose, just like a feather on a breeze, like a word wandering without any definite rhythms, like a weaving wandering line. The air's so gentle. It feels like Persephone's really on her way.

"Let's treat ourselves," says Mum. "Pizza? Or a Chinese to carry home?"

She looks at the menu of Wok This Way.

"Fried King Prawns in Kung Po Sauce!" she says. "Spring Rolls! Pork Cha Sui!"

I look at Pani's.

"Spaghetti Pomodoro! Pizza Quattro Stagione!"

She laughs and guides me to the door of

Pani's Pizza & Pasta Place. A waiter greets us like we're long-lost friends. He calls us two fine ladies. He gives us both a red rose. We sit at the back of the restaurant, the only ones at first, then other little families and couples start coming in. Music's playing, someone singing "O Sole Mio."

She sings quietly along for a line or two.

I order a pizza margherita with anchovies and olives and garlic.

Mum orders angel-hair pasta with clams and shrimps.

We grin at each other. She drinks white wine. I drink lemonade.

The food comes and is delicious.

"Fantastico!" she sighs.

"Marvelloso!" I say.

"O sole mio!" she quietly sings.

The day continues to darken outside.

I have pistachio and strawberry and vanilla ice cream. Mum has Panna Cotta con Caramello.

"For the sound of it as much as the taste of it," she says. "Say the words: Panna Cotta con Caramello."

We say the words together. With two long-handled spoons we eat the sweets together. We sigh at such deliciousness.

Mum drinks coffee, then we go out into the gathering night. We retrace our steps towards home, go down into the park again. We follow the stream. We hear birds settling down in the hedges and the undergrowth. A couple of cats, black beasts, are prowling, hunting.

We sit on a bench by the stream in the dark.

"That was lovely, wasn't it?" says Mum.

"Delicioso!"

"And the walk? And the visit to Dad?"

"Fantastico!"

"You are OK, aren't you?"

"Yes, mostly."

"Mostly's pretty good."

She puts her arm around me. We watch the stars intensify. We stand up and slowly walk on. We follow the footpath.

"When you grow up," I said, "do you ever stop feeling little and weak?"

"No," she says. "There's always a little frail

279

and tiny thing inside, no matter how grown-up you are."

"Like a baby?" I say.

"Yes. Or like a tiny bird, right at the heart of you," she says. "It's not really weak at all. If we forget it's there, we're in deep trouble."

We walk on, heading for the gates, but she takes my hand and turns me away from the path.

We walk to the darkest part of the park, beyond the swings and the bowling green. A few lights mark the pathways behind us. Lights from Crow Road and Falconer Road and from the city twinkle through the trees. The night's dead still. I think again of the Underworld, and I shudder, then I turn my thoughts away. I feel the solid earth under my feet. I feel the air on my skin. I lift my eyes to the sky, to the millions of stars.

Mum shows me Saturn and Venus. She points out the constellations: Virgo, Cancer, Leo. She shows me the cluster of the Pleiades. We try to look further, further, through the stars that are scattered like dust across eternity. We try to make out the beasts and weird winged beings that the Greeks described up there: bears and dogs and horses and crabs and Pegasus and Daedalus and Icarus. We imagine a sky filled with beasts and beings.

"We're looking across billions and billions and billions of miles," she says. "The light from some of the stars has taken millions of years to reach us."

"We're time travelers!" I say.

"Yes."

"And we're made of the same stuff. The stars and us."

"Yes. No matter how far away we are from each other."

We stand dead still and we listen to the night. The city drones. An owl hoots and a cat howls and a dog barks and a siren wails.

We let the stars shine into us.

I stare. Is there anyone else out there? There has to be. Are they like us? Is there another Mina and another Mum looking toward us through the darkness that goes on for billions and billions and billions of miles and billions and billions and billions of years? Are their joys and their pains the same as ours? Will we ever know the answers to things like that? And how did everything get here, anyway? And why? And will it go on forever? And what's right out there at the very edge of the stars and the darkness? And what's at the very heart of things?

Mum cups her hands around my head.

"Look," she murmurs. "I can nearly hold your whole head in my hands, Mina. Your head holds all those stars, all that darkness, all these noises. It holds the universe." She holds me against her. She rests her head against mine. "Two heads, two universes, interlinked."

After a while, we make our way back towards home. She holds my hand as we walk and she's happy at my side.

We hold each oth-er's hand and walk back home

We walk back home and hold each oth-er's hand

We...

We come to a lamp beside the pathway, and suddenly we stop our walking, and we start to dance, and we glitter in the shafts of light, like stars, like flies, like flakes of dust.

EXTRAORDINARY ACTIVITY

Take a line for a walk.

Find out what you're drawing when you've drawn it.

Take some words for a walk.

Find out what you're writing when you've written it.

Take yourself for a walk.

Find out where you're going when you get there.

EXTRAORDINARY ACTIVITY

Stare at the stars. Travel through space and time.

Hold your head and know that you are extraordinary.

Remind yourself that you are dust.

Remind yourself that you are a star.

Stand beneath a streetlamp.

Dance and glitter in a shaft of light.

EXTRAORDINARY ACTIVITY

Listen for the frail and powerful thing at your heart.

A DREAM
OF HORSES

Later, just before I go to bed, I look out of the window. There are lights on in the house I still call Mr. Myers's house. Shadowy figures move behind the windows. I think of the baby and hope that she's sleeping peacefully. I keep the curtains open. The moon rises and its maddening light falls on me. I tremble. Does everybody feel this excitement, this astonishment, as they grow? I close my eyes and stare into the universe inside myself. I feel as if I'm poised on the threshold of something marvelous. I drift to sleep at last.

I dream. Such a weird dream! I see the night sky filled with beasts and extraordinary beings, all the beasts and beings imagined throughout history. As I stare up to watch them, they start to fall towards me.

I DREAMED OF HORSES

I DREAMED OF HORSES FALLING FROM THE SKY
I DREAMED OF SERPENTS FALLING FROM THE SKY
I DREAMED OF BEARS AND GOATS AND CRABS
AND LIZARDS FALLING FROM THE SKY.
I DREAMED OF CENTAURS, OF PEGASUS
OF DAEDALUS AND ICARUS
FALLING FROM THE SKY.
I DREAMED OF THE ARCHAEOPTERYX
FALLING FROM THE SKY.
I DREAMED OF OWLS AND LIONS
BATS AND BULLS AND FISH
AND RAMS AND ANGELS
FALLING FROM THE SKY.

AND ALL THE HORSES AND THE SERPENTS
THE BEARS, THE GOATS, THE CRABS AND LIZARDS
THE CENTAURS AND THE LIONS
AND PEGASUS AND DAEDALUS
AND ICARUS AND ARCHAEOPTERYX
AND OWLS AND BATS AND BULLS AND FISH AND
RAMS AND ANGELS
LANDED IN MY ROOM
AND GATHERED BY MY BED
AND WHISPERED IN MY EAR
WAKE UP, MINA. WAKE UP. IT'S TIME TO WAKE.

And I wake. And it's dawn. And I'm still so close to the dream that I can nearly hear the snorting and the stamping and the rustling of wings, I can nearly feel the heat of the beasts by my bed. Then the after-dream disappears and there's just me and the room and silence. But not true silence. There's the drone of the city. There's the beat of my heart. There's Mum breathing gently in the room next door.

I go downstairs. Make chocolate milk and toast. Delicious. Go to the front door and stand there. The street's empty, just cars lined up against the curbs. The sky's empty, just a few clouds and passing birds. The dream repeats in my memory and the sky is filled again for a moment with falling beasts. I sip the lovely chocolate. I listen to the birds, to the dawn chorus, to what might be the voice of God.

I move to the tree, and I stand beneath it, against the trunk. The blackbirds squawk, but they know it's only me and they soon calm down. I close my eyes and listen closer, deeper. And I hear the sound I want to hear, tiny and distant, as if it's from another world. It's coming from the nest. It's the sound of tiny cheeping chicks. I smile. And then there's another sound, just as tiny, just as far away, just as urgent.

The baby crying.

Suddenly, the miserable-looking doctor drives into the street in his miserable-looking car. He pulls up at the house just as he did when it was Mr. Myers's house. He scans the street with his miserable-looking eyes, then the door's opened to him and he goes inside. Then a nurse appears, walking quickly, much too quickly, from the end of the street, and goes into the house, too.

I listen. No sound. Just my heart, just the chicks, just the city.

Then Mum's at my back.

"Mr. Myers's doctor's come," I tell her.

"Mr. Myers's doctor?"

"Yes. For the baby."

"You can't know it's for the baby."

"A nurse came, too."

"A nurse? It's just routine, I'm sure it is."

"I heard the chicks," I tell her. "Then I

heard the baby crying."

As we stand, another car pulls up. Another nurse goes in. I chew my lip. I tremble slightly. It's so weird. I feel like I've just been born myself, as if I'm at the edge of a huge adventure. But the doctor's face. And the nurse's. And the lines of worry on Mum's brow.

"It's probably nothing," she says. "Little baby, a few days old."

The blackbirds squawk. I see Whisper prowling in the shadows below the garden hedge. I hiss. I wave him off. He slinks backwards, further into the dark. But his eyes continue to shine from there.

Mum draws me back inside. We eat toast and drink tea. I keep going to the front window. An hour passes. More. Then the first nurse comes out and walks away. I tell Mum. She comes and we watch again. Then the other nurse comes out. She looks at her watch, rubs her eyes, gets into her car, drives away.

But no doctor. Nobody else.

"If we were outside we'd be able to listen for the baby," I say. "We'd be able to hear if she's OK."

"It will be OK. Sometimes getting into the world safely can be difficult, that's all."

I see Whisper slinking out from the shadows, turning his ear towards the nest. I tap on the window. I bare my teeth. He looks at me, decides to ignore me, and slinks forwards again.

Then at last the doctor comes out. He stands with the dad at the door and they shake hands. He casts his miserable gaze along the street and drives away.

"Thank Heaven," says Mum. She sighs with relief. "It must have been nothing."

"Nothing," I echo.

I hiss at Whisper.

"No!" I tell him. "No!"

She looks at her watch.

"I'll go along later, see if I can help."

I sit by the window and take a pencil for a walk across a page.

Hours pass. Mum walks along the street

toward the house, but I see her quickly turn back again.

"What's wrong?" I say.

She shrugs.

"They sound rather ... agitated. Not surprising, I suppose. I'll try again later."

The boy comes into the street. Clenched fists. Hard eyes. He has his football. He kicks it against the wall. He goes back in again.

"He'll need a friend, you know," she says.

"Will he?"

"Wouldn't you?"

She leaves me.

I take my pencil for another walk across the page. I tell myself the page is the street, the pencil is me, walking closer to Mr. Myers's door.

I feel so stupid, so nervous, so young. I've never once gone out and tried to make a friend before.

I take deep breaths.

I write.

Mina McKee walked along the street and knocked on the door and the boy came and Mina said, "Hello. My name is Mina. What's yours?"

Do I dare? I imagine him in the house, gloomy and surly. I imagine him coming to the door and glaring at me and telling me to go away. What would a boy with a football under his arm want with somebody like me?

But writing it makes me bolder.

Mina got up and went out of her front door and walked along the street. Mina got up and went out of her front door and walked along the street.

Maybe he wouldn't be gloomy. Maybe he'd really be glad. Maybe he would want something to do with somebody like me.

I get up. I put the book and the pencil down. I go out of the door. I walk along the street. My heart's thudding. The air's dead still. I hear yelling, the kind of yelling Mum must have heard. It comes from the back of the house. A woman's voice, angry and scared. I don't turn back. I quickly walk to where the houses end, then turn into the lane that runs along the back of them. I come to the back of Mr. Myers's house. There's an ancient derelict garage there. The doors to the lane must have fallen off years ago and there are dozens of massive planks nailed across the entrance. Next to the garage there's a six-foot-high wall. There's a waste bin against the wall. I could easily get onto that and then to the top of the wall and look down into the garden and say, "Hello. My name is Mina."

The woman yells again.

"Keep out! All right?"

I hear the boy muttering something. It just seems to make her angrier.

"Do you not think we've got more to worry about than stupid you?" she yells. "So keep out! All right? All right?"

She sounds so scared, at her wits' end.

"Just keep out!" she yells again, then it's silent.

I stand in the lane all alone. I tell myself

I should go back home, but it feels like an adventure to be standing there, even though I'm so close to home, even though everything's so still and so silent. My heart beats fast.

Soon I hear the boy kicking the ball. I lean against the garage and feel it trembling as the ball thumps against it. Thump! Whack! Thump! I hear the boy's grunts of effort and frustration. Who is he? What'll he be like if I'm brave enough — when I'm brave enough to speak to him?

After a while, there's his mother's voice again. Will he come in for lunch? *No*, he tells her. *No!* Then I hear their voices close together. She's calmer now. I imagine her at his side, touching him, tousling his hair, reasoning with him, explaining her anger. It's the garage she's scared of. It must be. Please keep out of it, she must be telling him. Then I hear a doorbell, and her feet hurrying away. *Now!* I tell myself. *Now!*

But I don't. Do it! I tell myself, but I don't. And there's the creaking of a door, then silence again. No football. And then his dad's voice, yelling, too.

"Michael! Michael! Didn't we tell you ...."

Michael. That's his name. But it's too late.

He's with his dad now, and his dad thumps a wall and the garage shudders and I hear them heading back towards the house.

Silly Mina! Lost your chance! Chicken!

I wait, but they've gone. And I trail back home. And I write again.

Chicken! I'm frightened. Don't be frightened!

I try not to feel silly and forlorn. I write an extraordinary activity for myself, the most important of all extraordinary activities. I pin it up above my bed.

EXTRAORDINARY ACTIVITY
BE BRAVE!

I read it and read it. I tell myself to be as brave as a chick making its first flight, as brave as Steepy with his tattoos, as brave as Sophie with her operation, as brave as Mum living without Dad, as brave as the baby leaping into the world. I write the words to help me.

Mina was brave and she tried again. She walked along the street and into the back lane. She stepped up onto the waste bin and then up onto the wall and she said, "Hello. My name is Mina. What's yours?"

And I do it, just like that, the very next day.

I see him go off to school in the morning. I'm in the tree when he comes back in the afternoon. I don't wait long. I take myself for a walk into the back lane. I hear the boy and his dad talking together. Then his dad goes away. And I wait. And there's silence, just the creaking of a door, so he must be in there again.

As soon as he comes out! I tell myself.

I wait.

The creaking of the door.

Now! Do it!

I jump up onto the waste bin and look down from the top of the wall.

"Are you the new boy here?" I say.

He turns around, looks up, and at last I tell him in my brightest voice:

"My name is Mina!"